SIVIDIOUS STARK

and the
Stadium Between Worlds

For Wayne,
Follow your heart
and you will find
the magic.

48/50

SIVIDIOUS STARK

and the
Stadium Between Worlds

a novel
Greg Park

Covenant Communications, Inc.

Cover image by Jennifer Eichelberger. For more information, visit www.jenart.com.

Cover image and design copyright © 2013 by Covenant Communications, Inc.

Published by Covenant Communications, Inc.
American Fork, Utah

Printed in the United States of America
First Printing: February 2013

18 17 16 15 14 13   10 9 8 7 6 5 4 3 2 1

ISBN 978-1-62108-273-6

For Collin

Prologue
SACRIFICE

THE CHEMISTRY LAB AT SILVER City University was quiet save for the hum of machines. The worktables were clean and sparkling. Student experiments had been tucked away until tomorrow. The students themselves had returned to the dormitories to do their homework. Only Professor Raymond Stark remained, his face wrinkled in thought as he peered through a microscope at a chunk of mineral. Behind him, the dark of night pressed against the laboratory windows.

For the first time in his career, Dr. Stark had stayed late after teaching his classes. Normally, he went straight home to be with his family. The chunk of mineral he was studying through the microscope had forever altered that routine. Now he would never be able to go home again.

He shook the thought away and peered into the microscope once more. The mineral Veyonx was like none found on Earth, but he had seen it many times—long ago, before he had come to Silver City to work at the university. It was how he knew that the flickering pulses of light visible through the microscope were not electrical or magnetic in nature—they were magical. An extremely powerful magic to still be so visible in this world.

Dr. Stark let out a long, tired breath then glanced at the envelope the Veyonx had arrived in. His name was written on the front in two languages. The first was English. The second was a strange, spidery scroll he had almost forgotten how to read. Not that it would have mattered had he forgotten *all* the letters. The seal of the Kaladan Secret Police would have been enough to tell him they had finally caught up with him.

He shook his head in disbelief. The Kaladan Secret Police—the henchmen of those who ran the Games. Also called Agents, they were the enforcers of the twisted laws of the Kaladan. Their job was to hunt down those who had fled the Games in search of a better life.

He had no idea how they had found him after so many years, but he decided it didn't really matter. Once Agents knew where you were, you either fled to another world or you returned to the Games. And that was assuming they didn't just kill you outright.

Glancing again at the envelope on his desk, he frowned. The Veyonx, the spidery scroll, the Kaladan seal—all three together meant his pursuers wanted him to know they were coming for him. They wanted him to try to flee because it made the chase more entertaining for them. Perhaps they even wanted him to run home to check on the safety of his family.

He discounted the last thought as soon as it came. If they had known he had a family, they would have come for him at his home so they could capture his wife and children as well. And he would die before he let that happen. His only regret was that his family would never know the truth about his disappearance.

Peering into the microscope once more, he studied the pulses of magic flickering across the surface of the mineral. For the magic to still be so visible meant the Secret Police had arrived in this world only today. Probably this morning. Any earlier and the magic would have faded to almost nothing.

He looked at the clock and smiled. The Agents would have grown impatient by now. Soon their need to capture him would overcome their twisted desire for a footrace. It was going to be a pleasure to disappoint them. On both counts.

He removed the chunk of Veyonx from the microscope then moved to where he would have a clear view of the door and windows. "Come and get me," he said softly. "I'm tired of running."

Gripping the mineral tightly, he felt the magic within it. Felt it as he once had those long years ago before the Games had become corrupted and he'd been forced to flee his homeworld. The sharp edges of the mineral pressing into his palm gave him the courage he needed to stand his ground.

The Kaladan had made a mistake in sending this particular mineral. Not because he could access what remained of the magic—even though the laws of this world would still allow for that—but because of his knowledge of science. The science of this world, anyway, which was so different from the world the Kaladan inhabited that there was no way for them to know they had inadvertently given him a powerful weapon.

It was fortunate for him and everyone else in this part of the building that the young lady who had delivered the envelope hadn't dropped it. In this world, Veyonx was a hundred times more explosive than an equal amount of dynamite.

He would have allowed himself a chuckle, but footsteps sounded at the door. A loud hissing followed, and a bright green light shone beneath the door as his enemies used plasma cutters to slice through the lock. The door swung inward and three Agents of the Kaladan Secret Police moved inside.

The one who'd cut through the lock put the plasma cutter away and pulled a zobo stick from his belt. He pushed a button, and the stick flared to life with sizzling, blue electric energy. Holding it out in front of him, he joined the other two, who ignited their weapons as well.

Dr. Stark watched them warily, his eyes narrowed, his face set. As always, the Agents wore dark pants, dark hats and gloves, and dark trench coats. It was a surprisingly common look among many of the worlds they visited, and a casual observer might dismiss them as human. A closer look revealed blue-gray skin that was smooth but scaled like that of a trout. Their eyes, hidden now by dark glasses, were the yellow eyes and black, slitted pupils of a snake.

"*Koysin Droja'Stark*," one of them said, calling Dr. Stark by his former name. The Agent continued to speak, but the words were in the language of the Kaladan, so only part of what he said was understandable.

Dr. Stark wasn't listening anyway. He was more concerned about the sizzling energy of their zobo sticks than about whatever they might be telling him. Words were meaningless in light of a weapon that could disable or kill a man with a single touch. That the Agents had their weapons set to stun showed they wanted to take him alive.

He couldn't allow that to happen. His dealings with the Kaladan had convinced him that there were things even worse than death.

Steeling himself, Dr. Stark waited until the Agents raised their weapons to strike. Then, with a final prayer for his family, he dropped the chunk of Veyonx mineral at the feet of the Kaladan Secret Police.

1
SIVIDIOUS

STREAMS OF SUNSHINE BATHED THE toy TIE fighter in hues of orange where it hung suspended from the ceiling by fishing line. A short distance away, an X-wing banked toward it, its cannons wavering as the entire ship was rocked by a breath of warm air from a heat vent. An A-wing and TIE Interceptor held positions near the window, and a Colonial Viper and Cylon Raider were locked in imaginary combat near the bedroom door. A mechanized plastic solar system hung nearby, adding to the illusion of interstellar space as its planets rotated gently around a glowing yellow sun.

Posters covered the wall below the solar system—a periodic table, a map of the universe, an image of the Eagle Nebula taken by the Hubble Telescope—and magazine clippings from scientific journals filled the spaces around the posters. A poster featuring words of wisdom by Albert Einstein graced the far wall above a small dresser. Postcards from the Clark Planetarium and the Natural History Museum were pinned to either side. The dresser itself was cluttered with an odd assortment of rocks and minerals as well as beakers and tools from a chemistry set.

Next to the dresser stood a small writing desk, its surface covered with an assortment of scientific toys and gadgets. A plasma globe with flickering tendrils of lavender sat next to a red lava lamp, and a Galileo thermometer and barometer stood next to a Newton's cradle. There were magnets and gyroscopes and a glass drinking bird tilting down for a sip. A projection alarm clock shone the time on the wall above the desk, the glowing red image only slightly dimmed by the morning light. It was 6:44 A.M.

At 6:45 the alarm sounded, shattering Sividious Stark's dream and jolting him awake. Fumbling for the clock, he hit the button to shut off the alarm then flopped back on his bed. His heart was pounding, and he was hot and sweaty. The dream he'd been having—he supposed *nightmare* would be a better word for it—still flickered in his mind's eye. He pressed his hands against his face to make it go away.

When the images finally faded, Sividious let out a relieved breath and dropped his feet over the edge of the bed. He had dreamed about his father again. Dreamed about him working in his lab at the university when something had gone wrong with one of the experiments and everything had vanished into fire.

And this time, just like every other time he'd had the nightmare, he felt that his father's death might not have been an accident. It was foolish to think so, of course. But he simply couldn't get rid of the feeling.

After setting his Newton's Cradle in motion, he pulled on jeans and a white T-shirt bearing the symbol for pi then grabbed his backpack and headed to the kitchen for breakfast. His older brother, Sam, was there, already into his second bowl of cereal. Sam looked up as he entered.

"Hey, Siv," he greeted then nonchalantly tried to fold up the newspaper so Sividious couldn't see what was on the front page.

He needn't have bothered. Sividious knew what today was. He more than knew it—he felt it. It lay in his heart like a heavy, cold lump. He faked a smile.

"So, what did the media mongrels have to say about Dad?" he asked, tossing his backpack toward the door. "Did they spice up the carnage or what?"

Sam sighed. "No more than they usually do," he answered. "It's the fact that they felt the need to write about it at all that ticks me off. But I guess as long as there are newspapers and people to read them, the dead will never be able to rest." He pushed the paper toward Sividious. "Read for yourself."

University Explosion Still under Review

It has been one month since Professor Raymond Stark died in an explosion in his lab at Silver City University, and investigators still haven't determined the cause of the catastrophe. Equally baffling to investigators is the absence of Dr. Stark's body. Gavin Henderson, chief of Silver City's forensics unit, said, "Even with an explosion as intense as the one that destroyed the lab, we should have found something of the professor. But there was nothing. Not even a speck of DNA."

In an interview yesterday, Chief Henderson announced that his people have found two more anomalies with the explosion. The first is a chemical compound unlike any known to scientists. "But since we really only have the burnt residue of the compound," Henderson said, "it's unlikely we will ever determine what it is."

The second anomaly involves the remains of some kind of electronic device. Henderson said that its circuitry was extremely complex but had no identifiable power source. Henderson added that the FBI and the Department of Homeland Security have taken an interest in the findings, but he was unable to comment on what the findings might mean since the investigation has recently been classified. All evidence has been taken by the FBI for further analysis.

The $1.3 million reconstruction of the lab facilities at the university is underway. Students who have been forced to do lab work in other departments should be able to return to the lab by the beginning of the next school year.

Sividious tossed the paper on the table. "What's that crap about the Department of Homeland Security? Are they trying to say Dad was a terrorist or something?"

Sam shrugged uncomfortably. "Kinda looks like it, doesn't it? Especially with that talk of chemical compounds and electrical devices." He pushed the empty cereal bowl away. "What I want to know is why they've never mentioned it before."

"Because it was *classified*," Sividious grumbled.

"No," Sam said. "They said it has only recently been classified."

"What has?" a little voice asked, and Sividious and Sam turned to see Simone entering the room.

"Nothing," Sividious told her. "You wouldn't understand." He poured himself a bowl of cereal as he settled in at the table to eat.

Simone's eyes narrowed, and her jaw tightened. Turning up her nose at him, she put her hands on her hips. She might only be ten years old, but she had perfected the art of female drama. A high school girl who had just been dumped by her boyfriend couldn't have put on such a magnificent show.

"Is it about Dad?" she asked, her voice snippety.

Sam's face grew concerned. "What makes you say that?"

Simone's overly patient sigh was accompanied by the shaking of her head. "I'm not stupid." She moved to the table and sat down, folding her arms on the table and resting her chin on them. "Besides, Mrs. Panelli talked about it in school yesterday. She said today was the one-month anniversary of what would always be an important day in Silver City's history because of what happened to Dad at the university."

Sividious exchanged looks with his brother, but Sam shook his head. "It is an important day," Sividious told her. "It's the day Silver City lost the best science professor to ever live in this town."

Simone nodded, her face sad. "That's what Mrs. Panelli said too." Silence filled the room as the three siblings sat looking at one another, their moods dark as they thought about their father. Finally, Simone moved to the counter and retrieved her favorite box of cereal. Her face was troubled as she returned to the table and started to eat.

"Speaking of science," Sam said, obviously trying to change the subject, "isn't your presentation due next week, Siv?"

"Sure is," Sividious replied, unable to keep the excitement from his voice. "And I plan on getting the best grade in the class." He didn't like a lot of what happened at school, and a presentation in any other class would have made him want to stay home. But he absolutely loved science. It was the only class he actually looked forward to. The rest of his eighth-grade schedule he could do without.

"Don't you already have the best grade in class?" Simone asked, raising an eyebrow at him.

"Of course I do," Sividious told her. "And I want to keep it that way. Even more important, I want to one-up Kael Jensen and his group of moronic henchmen."

"Is Kael still picking on you?" Sam asked, his face hardening. He'd always been protective of his siblings, but since the death of their father, he'd been even more so. Sividious didn't mind having a live-in bodyguard, especially one who was six feet three inches tall, who weighed 235 pounds, and who played linebacker on Silver City High School's football team. He also liked how Sam's protectiveness made him seem very much like their dad.

"No more than usual," he answered. "But then Kael hasn't been able to prove it was me who turned his pee bright blue last week either." He started to laugh. "He came back from the bathroom crying like a little girl."

"Hey!" Simone shouted.

"No offense," Sividious said, putting up a hand to calm her. He started laughing again. "You should have seen it, Sam. Mr. Tough Guy himself running up to the teacher in a panic, bawling that his pee was blue and asking if he was going to die. I've never laughed so hard in my life. Neither had the class. Kael was so embarrassed that he didn't come back to school for two days."

"He'll beat the crap out of you if he ever finds out," Simone warned.

"He won't find out," Sividious assured them. "You are the only people I've told."

"Does he suspect you?" Sam asked.

Sividious shrugged. "Probably. But he'll never be able to prove it."

Simone leaned forward, her eyes twinkling with curiosity. "How did you do it?"

"Sorry. That's a trade secret."

Sam rose from the table. "Hurry up and get ready for school," he ordered. "The bus leaves in ten minutes."

"I don't ride the bus," Simone said.

Sam jingled keys at her. "Today you do," he said. "This bus leaves in ten. Mom left me the car."

"Sweet!" Simone shouted as she bolted from the room.

When she was gone, Sam took Sividious by the arm and looked him in the eyes. "You be careful today," he said, his face suddenly somber, "because Simone is right about what Kael will do to you if he finds out you're responsible for his embarrassment." He frowned. "I had a bad feeling about today before I learned about your prank—now I really feel like something bad is going to happen."

Sividious didn't know why, but Sam's words sent a shiver rushing through him. It settled in his heart like a lump of ice. He wanted to talk about the feeling with Sam, but Simone returned to the kitchen before he could speak.

"Let's go," Simone said excitedly then added, "I get to ride shotgun." Without waiting for a reply, she rushed out the door to the garage.

Sividious exchanged looks with Sam then followed his brother out the door.

The elementary school was a short three blocks from their house, so Sividious only had to endure the backseat for a minute. He climbed into the front as Simone ran across the playground to join her friends.

"Why did Mom walk to work this morning?" he asked.

Sam shrugged. "I don't know. She just popped her head into my room early this morning and said she didn't feel like driving." He glanced over with eyebrows raised. "You aren't complaining about not having to ride the bus to school, are you?"

"No. It's just . . ." He hesitated, searching for the right words. "What if the bad feeling you had earlier has something to do with Mom?"

"It doesn't," Sam said as he shook his head. "At least I don't think it does. I was about to blow it off when you told me about your prank on Kael." They stopped at a red light and Sam looked over at him. "You know it isn't wise to antagonize a bully, Siv. Kael already has it in for you. You shouldn't do things that will make him want to pound you even more."

"I have to do something," he insisted. "The guy is a jerk."

"But he is a very *large* jerk," Sam said.

Sividious snorted a laugh. "You got that right."

"Physically," Sam continued. "I'm serious, Siv. Kael is twice your size."

"But he only has half my brains," he countered. "Don't worry about it."

The light turned green, and Sam stepped on the gas, his face pinched into a frown at being brushed off.

Sividious watched him for a moment longer then turned and gazed quietly out the window at the buildings and streets slipping by.

Located high in the mountains of Utah, Silver City was really two towns in one. The historic mining district, with its antique, brick-front buildings and narrow streets, lay nestled at the foot of the mountains near the ski resort. The modern college town, with its strip malls, businesses, and industrial parks, spread across the valley to the east.

Of the two, Sividious liked the old mining town best, and he was glad his family lived in a neighborhood on the edge of the historic district. He liked the collection of rusty ore cars and other mining equipment on display in the park. He liked the old jailhouse and fire department museums. But most of all he liked the Silver City mine museum with its vast array of minerals, ores, and rocks.

His own collection was small by comparison, but he had a couple of pieces the museum didn't. It was something he liked to remind Mr. Griffen, the owner of the museum, about every time he visited.

"I'm going to drop the car off for Mom," Sam said as he pulled up in front of the junior high. "I don't want her walking home from work."

"Sounds like a plan," Sividious told him.

"Remember what I told you," Sam said. He still wore a frown, and there was worry in his eyes. "Stay away from Kael."

Sividious grabbed his backpack and opened the door. "Would you stop worrying?" he said. "I'll be fine."

2

AYA THE KELSPRITE

CLUTCHING HIS BACKPACK TO HIS chest, Sividious crouched farther into the undergrowth of Silver City's wilderness park and did his best to remain quiet. His breathing sounded loud in his ears as he peered out through the leafy green and prayed that Kael Jensen and his band of bullies wouldn't find him. He could hear them thrashing their way through the bushes somewhere to his left, calling for him to give himself up and promising not to hurt him.

Yeah right, he thought. Kael never let any of his victims go with anything less than a black eye or bloody nose. And right now Kael was even angrier than usual.

For the second time in a week Kael had lost face in front of his peers, and he wanted to punish the person he believed responsible for it. And Sividious had no intention of being pummeled simply because his newest form of scientific sabotage had given Kael a raging case of gas.

He knew Sam had warned him to stay away from Kael, and he had fully intended to do so. But when Kael had left his water bottle unattended during science class again, the temptation to act had been too hard to resist. So in spite of his brother's warning—not to mention his own better judgment—he had administered another round of justice with one little squirt of the dropper.

The mix of chemicals was totally harmless, of course, but the result was extremely alarming. Especially to the one who had just been turned into a human whoopee cushion.

Scared as he was of being thrashed for his antics, Sividious couldn't help but smile at the memory.

The moment of truth had come during history class. Kael's eyes went wide, and he asked Mrs. Andreason if he could be excused to go to the bathroom.

"You've already used all your bathroom passes," Mrs. Andreason said. "You'll just have to wait until school is out."

Face scrunched in discomfort, Kael looked at the clock and groaned when he saw that forty minutes remained. Ignoring everything but the explosion brewing in his guts, he squirmed in his seat for a full ten minutes before the laws of physics finally won out.

The first release of Kael's scientifically induced gas reverberated through the classroom like a jackhammer striking concrete and lasted a full fifteen seconds. The second turned Kael into an old car with a bad muffler as he bolted from the classroom in a panic.

The silence that followed was profound as every student in Mrs. Andreason's history class sat in stunned disbelief at the flatulent exhibition. And then someone snickered. It was followed by a giggle, then a chuckle. A moment later, every kid in class was laughing so hard it took Mrs. Andreason twenty minutes to quiet everyone down.

No sooner had she regained control than Kael returned with a note from the office. Working hard to maintain what was left of his dignity, he handed the note to Mrs. Andreason.

"I'm checking out," he said, then moved to his desk to retrieve his backpack. He left the room amid a chorus of muffled giggles and snickers.

As soon as he was gone, all-out laughter swept across the room, and Mrs. Andreason gave up on her lesson, unable to compete with the hysteria created by Kael's explosions. Sividious, however, had sat quietly during the entire episode, savoring the victory he'd won on behalf of all unfortunate enough to have been bullied by Kael. Which, when he looked around the room, was pretty much every kid in class.

But Kael hadn't gone home as expected. He'd waited out by the buses, rallying his fellow bullies and preparing to pound the person he thought responsible for his humiliation. It didn't matter that there was no evidence to prove Sividious had done it. If Kael thought you were guilty, you were guilty. End of story. Maybe even the end of your life.

Fortunately, Sividious's best friend, Jackie Molenshire, had seen what Kael was planning and had run back into the school to warn him of the impending ambush. Unfortunately, it was a three-mile walk home.

He'd made it as far as the wilderness park, a half mile short of his home, when Kael and five of his cretins had moved out of the alley next to the mine museum to block his way. They'd taken the bus to get ahead of him and had set up an ambush. As they'd moved to encircle him, Sividious noticed that Kael's face was a mask of rage unlike any he had ever seen before. Rage and a determination to thump Sividious to within an inch of the afterlife. Apparently the fear of dying of some dreadful urinary disease and today's gastric humiliation in front of the class had spawned a new level of aggression.

His own fear of dying had brought him to where he was now, hiding in the bushes of the wilderness park, well out of range of any adults who might hear him call for help. *Stupid, Sividious,* he thought. *Really stupid.*

He shook his head. He should have run into the museum. Mr. Griffen would have helped him. The old museum owner disliked Kael as much as Sividious did.

A rock crashed through the bushes, narrowly missing his head and startling him so badly he nearly jumped to his feet to run from his hiding place. But then he spotted the boy who had thrown the rock and realized the toss was just one of many random attempts to flush him out. They had no idea where he was. As long as he didn't move—

"There he is!" a voice shouted, and Sividious peered from the bushes to see Mike Wilson pointing at him.

Dang it! he thought and bolted from his cover.

He heard a hiss of rocks and flinched as they crashed through the trees and shrubbery all around him. One hit him in the back of the neck with a sharp, stinging pain that made his eyes water, and a second one glanced off the side of his head. It sent spots of light dancing through his vision and made his ears ring.

Prompted by the pain and fueled by his terror, he quickly outdistanced his pursuers but didn't stop even when he reached the end of the park. He climbed a chain-link fence and raced on into the true wilderness of the mountains surrounding Silver City, leaving the groomed trails of the wilderness park behind.

The scrub oak was thick and twisted and so dense he could barely make his way through it. The gnarled branches snagged his clothing and tore at his skin, and he shielded his face with his backpack to keep from losing an eye.

After forging his way through one particularly dense clump of oak, he found himself on a game trail. It was wide and inviting as it snaked upward through the dense undergrowth, and he took it without hesitation, eager to be away from Kael.

It wasn't until he reached the open area fronting the entrance to the abandoned silver mine that he realized he had gone much farther than he had thought. He paused, listening for sounds of pursuit. When he didn't hear any, he breathed a sigh of relief and moved farther into the open to look around.

Tailings covered most of the area—a gray, colorless field of crushed rock and ore that resisted even the most determined plants. Those that had taken root were spindly and looked sickly. Even sixty years after the mine's closure, the forest had been unable to reclaim the area.

Sividious made his way to the front of the mine and found a rusty ore car still sitting on a line of track exiting the mine shaft. He tried to push the car along the track, but its wheels were rusted in place.

Giving up, he turned to study the dark hole stretching into the mountain. Heavy timbers framed the cut in the rock, but they were weathered and looked to have lost much of their strength. It didn't take a genius to realize the Danger! No Trespassing sign was for real. It made him wonder why the city officials didn't just wall up the entrance completely.

The thought of being surrounded by all that stone and darkness gave him the heebie-jeebies, and he turned away. Moving back to the edge of the woods, he sat in the shade and waited until he was sure Kael and his band of thugs had given up the chase. When he was satisfied that they were gone, he cautiously made his way back down the game trail.

He was nearly to the fence separating the wilderness park from the rest of the mountain when frantic breathing sounded behind him on the trail. Whirling, he had just enough time to brace himself before a girl dressed all in blue plowed into him.

He caught her in his arms as they fell, and he did his best to keep her from getting hurt as they struck the ground. They tumbled into the tall grass near the fence, and the girl came to rest on top of him. Their faces were only inches apart as they stared into one another's eyes. Sividious was spellbound. The girl's eyes were the bluest he had ever seen. Even the whites of her eyes, or what should have been the whites, were blue. So were her skin, her lips, her hair, and her wings.

Wings!

Blinking in surprise, he pushed the girl off of him and scrambled to his feet.

The girl rose with him, making a calming gesture with her arms as her wings folded tightly against her back. They were long and slender but featherless, looking more like the wings of a bat or gargoyle than a bird. They reached nearly to her ankles. In spite of the wings and the strange color of her hair and skin, however, she was the most beautiful girl he had ever seen.

She was barefoot and wore a loose-fitting dress of blue silk that shimmered when she moved and ended well short of her knees. The only other thing she had on was a lanyard with an odd-looking badge on it. It looked like an ID badge for a company or business, but it had no picture and was covered with scribbled writing.

She wasn't real, he decided. She couldn't be. Blue girls with wings were creatures of fantasy and make-believe. He was either imagining all of this—a result of being hit in the head with the rock—or the girl was a fake, some weirdo who liked to dress up like a fairy creature.

Before he could decide which of the two it was, the blue girl started speaking in a language Sividious didn't understand. He listened for a moment, but it didn't sound like any language he'd ever heard at school or on TV. In fact, it didn't sound like a real language at all. It was filled with clicks and buzzes and hums, and it made the girl sound more like an insect than a person.

He shook his head at her. "I can't understand you," he said, then added under his breath, "And I'm not sure I want to."

She frowned at him, then removed the lanyard and offered it to him. When he hesitated, she took a step forward and forced it into his hand, motioning him to put it on even as she continued to chatter in her bizarre language. She spoke urgently, nervously casting his eyes about the woods while she waited for him to comply.

What could it hurt? he thought as he slipped the lanyard over his head. As soon as he did, the girl's words became clear.

"I don't have much time," she said. "Kaladan Agents followed me through the portal. They are not far behind. The lanyard you wear is theirs. I stole it from them in order to escape the stadium. As you can see, it allows you to understand me. It is an All Access Pass. Very rare and very valuable. It allows the wearer to enter the stadium through any one of its portals. It also allows access to all areas of the stadium, even those restricted to only the Kaladan and those who serve them."

"Uh," Sividious began, "are you all right? You didn't hit your head when we fell, did you? Because if you didn't, then you are crazier than I first thought. Especially if you think I'm going to play along with . . ." he hesitated, "with whatever it is you're playing."

She shook her head and motioned at the lanyard. "I can't understand you now that I'm not wearing that," she told him. "So be quiet and listen to me. I don't have much time." She shot a quick look back up the game trail for emphasis.

"The magic of this world is weak, so I cannot defend myself against the Agents. They will find me, and they will take me back to the Games. That is if they don't send me to work in the mines on the Kaladan home-world."

She took a step forward and looked him squarely in the eyes. "I don't know why I chose the portal to this world. I don't know who you are or if you can help me. What I do know is that I won't last another week if the Agents take me back to the Games. I'm tired of competing. I'm tired of being part of their twisted enterprise. If you can't help me, please find someone who can."

Harsh, guttural voices sounded on the slopes above them, and the girl's eyes went wide with fear. "They have found me," she said. "Remember what I have told you."

Sividious started to remove the lanyard, but she grabbed his arm to stop him. "The lanyard is yours now," she told him. "You will need it if you are going to help me." She pushed him away. "Run now," she ordered. "Don't let the Agents find you."

The way she said it sent a wave of fear through Sividious, and he turned and bolted away down the fence line. He felt like a coward for running away, but he was so freaked out by what had just happened that he didn't care. He didn't stop until he hit a stand of oak so thick a mouse would have had a hard time moving through it. Even so, he pushed himself into the gnarled mess and hunkered close to the ground, breathing heavily and trying to decide if he was going crazy.

He pinched his eyes shut in denial. Blue girls with wings, lanyards that acted as translators, talk of magic and agents that hunted you to make you compete in games—none of it made any sense. It had to be a delusion, a hallucination brought about by being conked on the head by that rock.

A thought struck him and he frowned. Or it was a prank. Something Kael had orchestrated as a way of getting even with him. If so, it was a darn good one to have frightened him so badly. His frown deepened as he considered how thoroughly he'd just been duped. Kael and his buddies must be laughing their heads off.

He shook his head. The only problem with the theory was the simple fact that Kael wasn't smart enough to have come up with such a plan. He and his cronies had all the imagination of a fence post. No, this was someone else's doing. But whose?

Slipping free of the oak brush, he quietly made his way back along the fence. Whoever the pranksters were, they were likely having a hearty laugh at his expense. He wanted to know who they were so he could devise a suitable scientific reprisal. Blue urine and gastric explosions were just the tip of the iceberg compared to what he could whip up if he wanted to. He would never actually harm anyone, of course; it wasn't in his nature to be violent. But the recipients of his next prank were going to wish they'd been born without noses.

When he reached the spot where he'd left the blue girl, he found the area empty. He listened for sounds of laughing or talking, but the forest was quiet. *Too quiet,* he thought as a shiver of fear rushed through him. Even the birds and squirrels had stopped their chatter.

Moving to the game trail he and the girl had used earlier, he let his eyes move up through the forest. He could see the slender imprints of her bare feet in the soft earth, one set coming down and one set going back up. And there, tramped deeply into the trail all around the girl's slender tracks, were two sets of heavy boot prints. She hadn't gone back up the mountain alone.

He cast nervously about the area. Something dreadful had happened here, he realized. Something that made him think the girl had been telling the truth.

3
AGENTS OF THE KALADAN

SIVIDIOUS STARED AT THE THREE sets of tracks for several minutes, trying to decide what to do. He still wasn't entirely convinced the blue girl wasn't just some elaborate prank, but he had decided she wasn't a hallucination. He'd already pinched himself several times to make sure he wasn't dreaming.

Finally, not knowing what else to do, he started up the trail in the direction the girl and the boots had gone. He supposed it wouldn't hurt to find out who was behind all the weirdness. If it turned out that she was telling the truth . . .

He let the thought die. He had no idea what he would do if she had been telling the truth.

As he neared the open area fronting the mine, he slowed, peering cautiously through the trees to see what lay ahead. He spotted the rusty mine car and its length of track, but he couldn't see much more of the area than that. He did hear voices, though, coming from somewhere near the end of the track. There was a hint of movement through the trees.

Looking around the forest, he located another game trail. It stretched away to the right, curving up toward the voices. He took it, hunkering low to the ground as he quietly worked his way to where he could see who was speaking.

When they came into view, Sividious crouched behind a large pine and peered through the boughs. The blue girl was there, flanked by two men in dark clothes and trench coats. At least he thought they were men. Their skin was an odd grayish-blue color that shimmered whenever the sunlight hit it just right. Both wore lanyards and dark sunglasses, and both held a slender metal rod of some kind in one of their gloved hands. The rods had the appearance of a police baton but hummed with a sizzling blue energy that shouted of pain and death. Dressed as the men-things were, they looked more like spies than police officers.

Agents, the girl had called them. Agents of someone or something called the Kaladan.

Sividious flinched as a loud hum sounded from within the mine shaft and the dark opening went bright with a flash of light. A moment later, two more Agents strode out into the afternoon sunlight and moved to join the others. One of them placed a lanyard around the blue girl's neck.

Sividious shook his head. This was getting weirder by the second.

"You were foolish to flee to this world, Aya," the newly arrived Agent said. "Magic is weak here. And the only sentient life-forms are technologically primitive humanoids. You would have done better to flee to a world where you would have blended in. Portal A16, perhaps. Or Portal E15." He glanced at his companions. "Any of those worlds certainly would have made for a more pleasurable chase for my men."

"If you wanted a better chase," Aya sneered, "you should have left the portal to my homeworld unguarded."

The Agent smiled, showing a row of pointed teeth. "My apologies, but the Kaladan didn't want you running home to warn your people. It would have disrupted the work of our Talent Scouts. Several dozen are there right now searching for new recruits for the Games."

"Searching for new slaves, you mean," she hissed.

The Agent shrugged. "Some, perhaps," he said. "Many will be thrilled to compete."

Aya glared at him. "Only those who are as demented as you and your masters."

"It's what makes the Games interesting," the Agent said, smiling. "Some compete because they like the competition. It is a chance for them to exert their dominance and to show their prowess and power. Others compete out of fear. Fear of being harmed. Fear of being sent to the mines. Whatever the reason, they compete just as fiercely. Self-preservation is a powerful motivator." He reached out and ran a gloved finger down her cheek. "What is your motivation, Aya? Is it fear or a lust for power?"

Aya slapped him across the face so hard it broke his sunglasses and knocked the hat from his head. It fell away to reveal a hairless dome covered with a layer of fine, iridescent scales. A ridge of bone, like the spine of some prehistoric fish, divided the shimmering head into two halves, stretching from the top of the creature's forehead to the base of his neck.

The Agents flanking Aya raised their sizzling batons to strike her, but the Agent who'd been slapped waved them off.

"I think you just answered my question," he said but gave no indication as to what he thought the answer had been. Aya, for her part, simply glared at him as he removed his broken glasses and bent to retrieve his hat.

When th Agent straightened once more, adjusting the hat atop the ridge of bone, Sividious got a look at his eyes. They were yellow, and the pupils were slitted like those of a snake.

The sight sent a shiver through Sividious and chased away his doubts about the girl and her story. She was not part of some elaborate prank to get even with him. She was a real being from another world who was in real danger. And the danger was just as real for him if the fish-looking Agent things found out he was here.

He wanted to slip silently away and forget the whole thing, but he forced himself to remain where he was. If he was going to help her—and deep inside he had already decided he would—he needed to know what they planned to do with her.

"Since it appears you haven't lost your fighting spirit," the Agent told her, "you will be returned to the stadium." He paused, and his snake eyes narrowed menacingly. "For now. One more transgression and you will be sent to the mines on Kaladan."

She opened her mouth to respond, but the Agent grabbed her by the throat, moving so fast Aya had only enough time to blink before his fingers closed around her neck. The fish-faced creature squeezed, and Aya's wings flapped as she struggled for breath. She hammered on the Agent's wrist with her hands, trying to break free.

"Do not try my patience, little Kelsprite," he warned. "You are not so valued by the Kaladan that they would punish me for killing you." He thrust her away then nodded to one of his men. "Take her back to her holding cell," he ordered. "And start an investigation into how she escaped."

"Yes, sir," the Agent said and motioned Aya forward. She complied, head lowered dejectedly as she moved toward the entrance of the mine. After only a few steps, however, she opened her wings and leapt into the air, rising dozens of feet with each thrust of her wings. She was about to disappear over the rim of the forest when a sizzling blast of energy from one of the batons sent her crashing down through the treetops.

"Stupid girl," the head Agent growled. He turned his reptilian eyes on the other Agents. "Go get her," he ordered. "If she still lives, put her in her cell. If not . . ." He hesitated as if considering. "If not, then throw her body to the Krotan. It hasn't eaten for weeks. I'm sure a Kelsprite isn't much more than a snack, but I would hate for her to go to waste." His malevolent smile made Sividious shiver.

"What about the All Access Pass she stole?" one of the Agents asked.

The head Agent frowned. "What about it?"

"It hasn't been recovered. She didn't have it with her when we captured her."

"She must have tossed it into the forest," the other replied. "Find it."

"Yes, sir," the Agent replied, then he and one of the others went to retrieve Aya's body. They returned a short time later, dragging her limp form between them. Sividious held his breath as he waited for them to speak.

"She's still alive," one of them said as they neared.

Sividious relaxed. He didn't know why he should care so deeply about a creature he'd only just met, especially one that was so obviously *not* human, but the fact remained that he did. Aya needed his help. All he had to do now was figure out *how* to help her. *And that,* he thought glumly, *will not be easy.*

"She went down a trail over there," one of the Agents said. "We caught her near a fence at the bottom of the mountain. She either tossed the AAP into the woods or threw it over the fence as we drew near. Don't worry, we'll find it."

He and his companion started across the expanse of ore and rock while the head Agent and his companion carried Aya's body into the mine shaft. There was a hum and a sudden flash of light, then silence.

Sividious barely noticed, intent on staying out of sight as the other two Agents moved past his hiding place. When they had disappeared down the trail he and Aya had used, it suddenly occurred to him that they might see his footprints just as he had seen theirs. If that happened, they would know he was here.

Angry at himself for not thinking of it sooner, he rose from his hiding place and quietly moved to the trail the two Agents had just gone down. He could hear their voices receding into the distance.

So far so good, he decided.

Still, he wasn't going to take any chances.

Opening his backpack, he quickly dug through the contents until he found his gym shirt. Sweeping it back and forth across the trail, he erased his footprints as he backtracked through the oak brush. He didn't stop until he was looking at the rusty ore car from the other side of the expanse of tailings.

He took controlled breaths to still his nervousness and glanced occasionally at his watch as he waited to see if his efforts had been worthwhile. He hoped they had, because he had no desire to learn what a sizzling blast from one of the batons felt like.

An hour passed, and finally the two Agents emerged from the forest. They made straight for the mine without stopping, and he could tell by their frowns that they were angry.

They moved into the darkness of the mine shaft, and a moment later the strange hum sounded, followed by a flash of light and then silence.

Sividious sat where he was for another hour, watching the entrance of the mine, and trying to work up the courage to follow. In the end, discretion won out over whatever valor he had been feeling earlier, and he rose and hightailed it down a game trail and away from the mine.

He told himself it was because he needed to get home before dinner so as not to upset his mom. The real reason, however, was fear. He was terrified by what he had seen, and he was starting to question his own sanity. Everything he'd ever learned about science shouted that this was not real. It couldn't be real. He didn't want it to be real.

Besides, there would be plenty of time to search for Aya tomorrow . . . assuming he didn't give in to reason and disregard the entire thing.

And that, he thought with a bewildered shake of his head, *is sounding better by the second.*

4
DECEPTION AND EXPERIMENTATION

Sividious arrived home to the smell of chicken potpie, and he found his mother and siblings already at the table eating. His mind raced with thoughts of Aya, the All Access Pass, and the Kaladan Agents; but he had decided even before leaving the wilderness park that he would say nothing about any of them. There was no way his family would believe him. He still wasn't sure he believed it himself.

Tossing his backpack into the corner, he joined his family at the dinner table.

His mother raised an eyebrow at him as he took his seat, but she didn't scold him or complain about him being late. Julia Stark had never been one to yell at her children. She didn't have to. When she wanted, she could deliver a gut-wrenching reprimand with nothing more than a look. Fortunately this wasn't one of those times, which meant she wasn't overly concerned by his tardiness. She simply filled his plate and asked how his day had been.

He shrugged. "It was okay, I guess."

"And how was school? Anything exciting happen today?" The tone hinted that she already knew something concerning his escapade with Kael.

A quick look at Simone confirmed his suspicion. She smiled sweetly, a picture of innocence as she waited for him to speak. The innocence was feigned, of course—the little brat had snitched on him once again.

He looked quickly at Sam, whose slight nod further confirmed Simone's betrayal.

"School was okay," he said, turning his attention back to his mother. "I got an A on my essay for English class. And in PE I ran the mile in under six minutes."

His mother didn't seem impressed. "Was that before or after Kael Jensen found out that you turned his urine blue?"

"He has no idea it was me," he countered then cringed when he realized he'd taken the bait.

"So you did turn it blue," she said. This time it wasn't a question.

He nodded. "Yes. But I did it a week ago. I'm sure he's forgotten all about it by now."

"Obviously not," she said. "Why else would he be looking for you after school?"

Sividious's brow raised in surprise. "How did you know about that?"

"Jackie called a little while ago asking if you'd made it home alive," his mother answered. "She told me Kael had been looking to pound you."

Sividious shot Simone his best death stare, then calmly met his mother's gaze. "But she didn't say anything about the prank, did she?"

"No. Should she have?"

Sividious shook his head. "She has no idea it was me either." He glared at Simone again. "But even if she had known, I doubt she would have blabbed it to the world like someone else I know."

"Sividious," his mother said, her voice stern, "I thought we talked about this. You can't keep using science as your platform for pranks on your peers. You know your father wouldn't approve."

"Actually," he said sheepishly, "Dad was the one who taught me how to do most of them."

"Even the blue urine?"

"Nope. I learned that one on my own."

"I see," she said flatly. "Still, I don't want you using your knowledge of chemistry or any other science to play any more tricks on that boy. Or any other person, for that matter. You could really get in trouble for something like that."

Sividious raised an eyebrow at her. "Would you rather I toilet paper their house or throw eggs at them like normal kids do?"

"Normal kids don't do any of those things," she said sternly. "And neither will you." She paused. "Will you, Sividious?"

"No, I won't," he told her, doing his best to sound disappointed. Inwardly, he was pleased with the loophole she had given him. As he saw it, they were talking about the use of toilet paper and eggs; she'd said nothing about using scientific retribution. Sure, she'd said she didn't *want* him to do it, but she hadn't flat out forbidden it.

There was a long silence as they ate, and Sividious found himself thinking about Aya once again. He couldn't have imagined her, he decided. He had the All Access Pass she had given him as proof that she had been real. It was tucked away in his backpack for safekeeping.

And the Kaladan Agents, he thought with a shudder, had seemed real enough. So had the weapons they had used on Aya. He hoped she was all right. Being shot down and crashing through the treetops must have hurt her badly.

It was Sam who finally broke the silence. "If Kael comes after you tomorrow," he said, his voice hard, "I want you to call me on my cell phone. I'll come to the school and pick you up. I might even have a few words for the little punk."

"I appreciate the offer," Sividious told him, "but I'll need to handle things on my own. Eighth grade is bad enough as it is. I don't even want to imagine the kind of teasing that would result from you coming to save me. I'd never hear the end of it."

"Suit yourself," Sam said. "But the offer stands nonetheless."

Sividious's mom nodded. "Or I could call and talk to his mother."

"Are you kidding?" Sividious exclaimed. "That's even worse than having your big brother stick up for you. Kael would let the whole school know about the phone call. I'd never live it down." He shook his head. "An embarrassment like that would follow me all the way through high school."

"Whatever you say," his mother said and gestured toward his plate as she stood. "Don't forget to put your dishes in the sink," she told him, then looked at Simone and Sam to show she meant them as well. "If you have any homework, get it done before anything else. I'll be out working in the flowerbeds. I have some fall bulbs I want to plant." She put her plate in the sink and went outside by way of the pantry. Simone left a moment later, heading to the living room to do her homework. When she was gone, Sam turned his gaze on Sividious.

"So what did you do to Kael *today?*" he asked, putting up a hand to stop the denial Sividious was opening his mouth to give. "Save it," he ordered. "I saw the look in your eyes when you were talking to Mom. There was something you weren't telling her."

A lot of somethings, actually, he thought, then shrugged. "I gave him a raging case of gas," he said, hoping to downplay the incident. He also hoped that Sam wouldn't sense there was more he wasn't telling.

"Gas, huh?" he asked. "Is that all?"

"Is that all?" Sividious said, trying to sound offended. "I turn my nemesis into a whoopee cushion, and you ask, *Is that all?*"

Sam held up his hands in surrender. "I didn't mean it like that," he said. "I'm sure it was brilliant." He took his plate to the sink, then turned back to face his brother.

"What I meant," he continued, "is did anything else happen to you today? Anything that might explain the scratches on your hands and arms. You look like you lost a fight with a giant cat."

Sividious was quiet a moment, considering. He hated what he was about to do. "I spent three hours hiding in the oak brush above the wilderness park while Kael and his band of thugs looked for me," he said. "It wasn't all bad. While hiding, I met a blue alien girl with wings. She was pretty, but Kelsprites really aren't my type. It's probably for the best that she was captured by secret agents and taken back to her homeworld."

Sam shook his head in disgust. "Funny, Sividious," he grumbled. "Very funny. Look, if you don't want to talk to me about your problems with Kael, just say so." He started away but stopped short of entering the hallway leading to his room. "But in case you decide to listen to reason, I'll say it again. Stay away from Kael." Without waiting for a reply, he disappeared down the hallway.

Sividious sat quietly for a moment, picking at his food. He had spoken the truth, but the deception was just as complete as if he had lied. He knew it would be. Sometimes the truth was simply too bizarre to be believed.

Frowning his disgust at what he had just done, he stacked his plate in the sink with the others, cleared the rest of the dishes from the table, and grabbed his backpack on the way to his room. Once there, he sat on the edge of his bed and took a closer look at the All Access Pass Aya had given him.

It was about the size of a deck of cards and was made of some kind of hard plastic. It was smooth to the touch and mostly translucent. One side was covered with a black, spidery-looking writing that appeared to have been burned directly onto the plastic. It looked ancient. The opposite side was smooth, and he could see what looked like a microchip embedded inside the card. He looked for a way to open it so he could get a closer look at the microchip, but the plastic was a single, solid piece.

He put the lanyard over his head and stared down at the AAP centered on his chest. He knew it was only his imagination, but it suddenly felt as heavy as a mine car. "What are you going to do, Sividious?" he whispered quietly.

The only thing I can do, he answered mentally, knowing that it was crazy and stupid and would probably lead to a great deal of trouble.

But he didn't care. He was a scientist. He had an obligation to research any and all fields of knowledge, no matter how strange they might be.

Steps one and two of the scientific method were already complete. He had observed the blue girl and the Kaladan Agents, and he had formed his hypothesis that what he had seen was real. Step three required experimentation to see if his hypothesis was correct.

And the only way he could think to do that was to use the AAP.

5
A STADIUM BETWEEN WORLDS

SIVIDIOUS LAY AWAKE FOR MOST of the night, tossing fitfully as he waited for dawn to arrive. He was nervous and excited, worried, determined, and a dozen other emotions that warred with one another until he was one big, fidgeting mess tangled in his sheets. He tossed them aside and lay staring at the clock. 2:43 A.M.

He focused on the red glow of the digital numbers being projected on the wall and willed time to go faster. After what seemed like an eternity, the three turned to a four, and he shut his eyes in frustration.

This is taking forever!

He rolled onto his back and tried to relax. The silver mine wasn't going anywhere. Neither was the portal supposedly inside it. Aya was either a prisoner of the Kaladan somewhere beyond the portal or she was dead. The All Access Pass would take him there or it wouldn't. This whole crazy thing was either real or it wasn't.

And no amount of tossing and turning would change the state of any of those things.

He glanced at the clock out of habit, then turned away in disgust. 2:46. He needed to get some rest or he wouldn't be going anywhere in the morning.

Flopping over onto his other side, he put his back to the clock and closed his eyes. *Slow your breathing*, he told himself. *Relax your muscles and let yourself sink into the softness of the pillow. Clear your mind of everything. Feel the quiet.*

It worked, and he felt himself slipping toward sleep. He was almost there when an image of Aya flitted unbidden through the darkness creeping over his mind. His eyes popped open and his anxiety returned.

Crap!

Grabbing his pillow, he wrapped it around his head and clamped it down with his arms. He took control of his breathing and began to relax once more. A short time later he was asleep.

* * *

The sound of his alarm jolted him awake, and he looked over at it, fully expecting to see that only a few minutes had passed. It certainly felt like he'd just barely fallen asleep. His head was heavy and his thoughts groggy. One of his arms was asleep and tingled with that pins-and-needles feeling he hated. When his eyes finally focused on the numbers, he forced a tired smile. 6:45. Morning had finally arrived.

Smacking the snooze button, he lay back down and gazed up at the ceiling. He was anxious to get going for the day, but he had to play this right or he would be going to school instead of up to the mine. When your mother was a nurse, faking an illness was like trying to fake your death while lying on an operating table hooked to an EKG. And Julia Stark didn't need any high-tech devices; hers were built right in to what she called her "mother senses."

Seven minutes later the alarm went off again, and again he hit the snooze button. If his mother hadn't left early so she could walk to work like she had done yesterday, she should be in to check on him before the alarm sounded a third time.

Two minutes later she came into his room and put her hand on his head to check for a fever. *Regular as clockwork*, Sividious thought and waited until his mother's hand pulled away.

"No fever," she said. "Tell me what's wrong."

"Nothing," he said. "I just didn't sleep very well." He sat up and cringed when the inside of his head screamed in protest. He reached up and rubbed his eyes. "I do have a raging headache, though."

"Lack of sleep will do that to you," she said as she ran her fingers through his hair. "Is there anything in particular that kept you awake?"

He shook his head and immediately regretted the movement. "Not that I can put my finger on, no."

She smiled knowingly. "If you would like to stay home today and rest, that will be fine with me."

He stared at her, not quite sure he had heard her correctly. Never in the history of the Stark family had she given in so easily to an attempt to stay home from school. Either he looked as bad as the inside of his head felt, or she had reasons of her own for keeping him home today.

And then it dawned on him. She thought he was afraid to go to school because of Kael Jensen. He was, of course, but not enough to skip school. He'd been dodging beatings from Kael for years. The guy was big and persistent, but he was dumb. Unless one of his cronies did the dirty work for him, Kael would never catch him.

He studied his mother for a moment and realized that she was letting him stay home because *she* was afraid of what might happen if he went to school. She feared he might get pounded.

Finally, he lay back down. "Rest would be nice," he said, feigning a tired smile. He supposed it wouldn't hurt to humor her. Staying home from school was the plan, after all. If she thought he was afraid to face Kael, that was fine with him.

"Okay, sweetie," she said, bending to kiss him on the forehead. "I'll see you when I get home from work."

She returned to the kitchen, and the sound of voices reached his ears, muffled and indistinguishable. He did hear one word loud and clear, though: *faker.* That came from Simone.

He stayed where he was until the house was empty and quiet. When he was sure no one would be coming back for forgotten items, he rose and dressed. He emptied his backpack of all his school stuff—no need to lug around all those heavy books—then took some ibuprofen for his headache and packed himself a lunch and a flashlight.

Before he left, he wrote a note explaining that he was feeling better and had gone to do some research for his science project. It was true in a sense, he decided. It just wasn't a science project he would be presenting in school.

It took him less than twenty minutes to reach the fence at the back of the wilderness park, and he climbed it without hesitation. Anxious now, he made his way quickly up the game trail to the mine.

He passed the rusted mine car and made his way down the narrow track to the dark opening stretching into the mountain. He stopped, a wave of uncertainty washing through him. *What if it is real?* he wondered. *What then*?

Pursing his lips in determination, he pulled the lanyard from his backpack and put it on then gazed down at the All Access Pass on his chest. It was time to test his concept of reality.

The air inside the mine was decidedly cooler than the air outside, and it smelled of rotting wood and damp, musty earth. He hesitated, momentarily afraid to continue, but after a few deep breaths, he forged onward. It grew dark after only a few paces, so Sividious pulled the flashlight from his backpack and clicked it on.

The narrow beam stretching away down the mine shaft only emphasized the depth of the darkness; it seemed to go on forever. He shined the light on the rail tracks in front of him and along the walls to either side. There was nothing to indicate this was anything other than an abandoned mine. Still, he supposed it wouldn't hurt to go a little bit farther.

Aiming the flashlight at the ground in front of him, he started forward again.

The interior of the mine flashed a brilliant white, and Sividious found himself standing in a dimly lit corridor that appeared to be made of plastics and polished metals. A short distance ahead, a larger corridor intersected the one he was in, but it too was dimly lit and appeared empty.

So, it is real, he thought, then clicked off his flashlight and stood there in silent wonder. *But where am I?*

A glance over his shoulder revealed a shimmering door of . . . of . . . something. It looked like water, but it was as dark and depthless as the mine had been. It was set in a metal framework rimmed with blinking lights. He studied the shimmering surface for a moment but had no idea what it might be. When he poked it with his finger, he was rewarded with a series of ripples that gave off a slight humming sound as they moved outward toward the framework.

A wormhole, he thought, *or something like it. Einstein was right*.

Under normal circumstances, the thought of his favorite scientist's theory being right would have made him happy. Right now it served only to scare the crap out of him because it meant he was no longer on Earth. He might not even be in the same galaxy anymore. It was enough to make him want to leap back through the wormhole—the portal, Aya had called it—and never return.

He stopped himself by sheer scientific will. There was too much to learn and too many things for him to discover to run home like a frightened kid. He doubted Albert Einstein would have left after learning his theories were correct. He nodded, knowing that he owed it to the scientific community to learn more about this place. He owed it to his father. He owed it to himself.

And now that he knew she was real and had been telling the truth about this place, he owed it to Aya. He needed to help her escape from the Kaladan and their fish-faced Agents.

He backed away from the shimmering portal and studied the sign on the wall above it. The markings were similar to those on the All Access

Pass—a spidery scroll that looked more like symbols than actual letters—so Sividious was surprised when he found that he could read them. Their meaning just popped into his head as if he were reading English.

Portal T16.

So, the All Access Pass lets me read languages as well as hear them, does it? Awesome. He lifted the AAP and looked at the side marked with the strange, scribbled writing. K345-876-GCP.

"Probably a serial number," he said quietly, then turned his back on Portal T16 and moved down the narrow passage until he reached the larger corridor. A quick look in each direction showed that the way was clear, so he turned right and continued cautiously forward. The corridor was wide and curved slightly to the left as it stretched into deepening shadow.

On his right, passages similar to the one leading to Portal T16 were spaced at regular intervals. He read *Portal S16* above the closest one and *Portal R16* above the one beyond. To his left the passages were shorter and seemed to open into a stadium of some kind. He could see what looked like bleachers silhouetted against a backdrop of stars. The sign above the nearest passage read *Concourse S16.* On each side of the concourse, the square outlines of concession stands were closed against the night, their gates lowered and their menus dark. He noticed rectangular openings along the walls at regular intervals. Labeled *Refuse*, they glowed red with scorching heat. Incinerators, he realized, and thought about how handy one would be back home. He'd never have to take out the trash again.

Moving to the concourse, Sividious crept forward until he could see into the stadium. What he found took his breath away. The night sky was filled not only with stars but with galaxies. Dozens of them. Their spiral and elliptical shapes were clearly visible. They were of various sizes and colors—some white, some blue, some pink—but each shone with a brilliance that made him think if he stretched out his arm he might touch them.

He shook himself free of the spell the wondrous sight had put upon him and turned his attention to the stadium itself. It was larger than any sports arena he'd ever seen on Earth, at least ten times that of the Rose Bowl, and had a tower of box seats on one side and massive video screens opposite the tower and at both ends. The field itself was several hundred feet down—some fifteen levels or so—and was lost in darkness.

Sividious shook his head in awe. What a sight the place must be when filled with hundreds of thousands of spectators. He suddenly wondered how many of those spectators were people like himself and how many were creatures like Aya and the Kaladan Agents. He imagined it would be like a scene out of a *Star Wars* movie, with creatures and beings of every kind and shape. As cool as it sounded right now, he didn't think he actually wanted to witness such a sight until he had come to terms with everything else he had learned so far. There was only so much weirdness the human mind could take before it freaked out. And he was already freaked enough as it was.

He looked back up at the galaxies filling the night sky. *A stadium between worlds,* he thought. And not just a few worlds either. Dozens of galaxies' worth of worlds. He shook his head. But how was it possible for so many galaxies to be visible so close together? Where was this place?

Blowing his cheeks out in bewilderment, he stared at the spirals of light until the immensity of space began to weigh heavily upon him, making him feel small and vulnerable. When he could stand it no longer, he turned his back on the canvas of stars and retreated into the darkness of the stadium's main passage.

He'd seen the worlds from a distance—he supposed it wouldn't hurt to experience a few of them firsthand. What was a trip into another galaxy when one had already left his own? And he had left it, he realized. This stadium—this in-between place of portals and bleachers and concession stands—was just that: an in-between place. It was part of all the worlds and yet not really part of any. He got the feeling that if he were able to look over the top edge of the stadium he would see nothing but the vastness of space stretching away to infinity.

If given the chance, he decided it was a sight he would like to see. First, though, he wanted to investigate a portal or two.

6
THE PORTALS

BACK IN THE MAIN PASSAGE, Sividious continued down its length, perusing the concession stand menus and trying to work up the courage to enter a portal to see what kind of world lay beyond. As he walked, he discovered that some of the portal entrances were blocked by energy fields, sizzling sheets of blue-green energy that looked as if they would fry any would-be trespasser the way a bonfire would fry a gnat.

He suspected the All Access Pass would allow him entrance, so he tested the theory by approaching one of the shielded doors. As expected, the sheet of energy dissipated, but he didn't enter. If the Kaladan felt it necessary to keep a portal closed, there was probably a good reason.

Continuing on, he made it all the way to Portal J16 before he finally worked up the courage to visit another world. It would be a quick peek, he told himself. He would step through the portal, look around, and then step back into the stadium. Simple.

He moved down the narrow passage leading to the portal and stopped in front of the shimmering wall of whatever-it-was. The lights in the metal framework surrounding the portal began to blink faster in response to his approach, and the portal itself began to hum. He stepped through.

Brilliant light enveloped him for one brief moment, and he found himself standing in a stone courtyard fronting a pyramid-shaped building. He stood just outside the building, beneath a stone arch marking the entrance. A thick forest surrounded the courtyard, and vines and lace-leafed ivy crisscrossed the stonework in many places. The sounds of birds and other forest creatures filled the air. A gap in the trees at the far end of the courtyard showed where a wide path descended to somewhere below.

Sividious glanced around cautiously, then moved across the courtyard to where he could see down the path. He found that it was actually a set of stairs. They dropped away at a very steep angle, ending at a broad meadow a hundred or so yards below.

He was about to go down the stairs to get a glimpse of what lay beyond the forest, but a loud howl sounded from somewhere in the meadow below. It was hungry and feral and made the hair on the back of his neck stand on end. It reminded him of the roar of the T. rex in the movie *Jurassic Park.*

He was so surprised by the sound that for a moment he couldn't move. Then something big and dark moved past the opening at the bottom of the stairs, and Sividious turned and hightailed it for the stone pyramid. He plunged through the entrance in a flash of white and found himself back in the passage of Portal J16.

"Mental note to self," he said quietly. "Don't go back to that world."

When he reached the main corridor, he decided to go right once more. If the Kaladan language had the same number of letters in its alphabet as English, then he should be about halfway through it. If not, and there were more, he could always turn around and go the other way. He would know soon enough—he had just passed Portal D16.

Portal C16 was shielded by the same sizzling energy field that had shielded earlier portals, but Portal B16 was open. So was A16. He moved past them both without stopping, anxious to see if there were only twenty-six letters to the Kaladan alphabet. Would it jump back to Z, or would there be some other letter? He was about to find out.

The sign came into view, and Sividious breathed a quick sigh of relief when he read Z16 above the corridor entrance. He wasn't sure why he was so relieved, but he suspected it was the need for normalcy in an otherwise bizarre place.

Turning into the narrow passage, he decided to see what the world beyond Portal Z16 looked like. He approached the shimmering doorway without hesitation and stepped through in a flash of white.

A blast of cold wind took his breath away, and pellets of snow and ice lashed at him in a blinding white fury. He put his hands up to shield his eyes, but there was nothing but a sea of snow. The entire world was lost in white.

Well, this stinks, he thought and quickly stepped backward through the portal.

Shaking the snow from his clothing, he turned his back on Portal Z16 and vowed never to return. Living in the mountains of Utah, he saw his fair share of snow every winter. No need to experience it more than he had to.

He shook his head. Maybe Portal Y16 would have a more favorable climate. *And be free of giant monsters,* he added. He certainly hoped so. He didn't like the idea that every world might be as inhospitable as the first two he had visited.

Bracing himself for another disappointment, he stepped through the shimmering wall.

It was dark on the other side of the portal, and walls of concrete and steel rose above him to the left and right, stretching so far into the night sky that they seemed to merge into one. Trash littered the ground around him, and the charred and twisted shell of some kind of vehicle hunkered near the building to his left. He heard the scurrying of clawed feet and caught glimpses of what looked like rats fleeing into the shadows. The far end was bright with lights and blurred movement. Sounds of traffic echoed toward him.

He was deep inside an alley, he realized, turning to look behind him. A dead-end alley that was part of a very large and busy city. And if the burned-out vehicle meant anything, it was a not-so-friendly-looking city as well. He studied the area a moment longer to make sure he wasn't in any immediate danger, then crept cautiously forward, determined to see what lay beyond the confines of the alley.

What he found took his breath away, and he stopped well within the alley's concealing shadows to take it all in. Vehicles of every shape and size streamed by to the hum of fiery-blue engines. Some were open to the air, the occupants visible. Most had enclosed cockpits of shaded glass. Not a single vehicle had wheels.

Contrary to what he had expected to find, there was no street beyond the alley, just a railed, narrow pedestrian walkway fronting the buildings. And beyond that short railing, the alley dropped away into a concrete channel that stretched as far down as it did up. And level after level was filled with a dizzying stream of airborne traffic, with hundreds of thousands of aircraft that defied everything he knew about the laws of physics.

If George Lucas could see this, he thought, marveling at how much it looked like the cityscape of Coruscant from the *Star Wars* movies.

He moved to the railing and looked down at the seemingly bottomless depths of the street and the never-ending stream of traffic. He shook his head in wonder. *How tall is this building?*

The sound of voices reached his ears, and he looked up to see several creatures on the level above him. They were shaped like human beings but were far too tall to be human. They also had two sets of arms and bright red skin with grayish stripes covering their faces. They were leaning out over the railing so they could see him, and two were waving to get his attention. He could just make out what they were saying.

"You fool! You can't be on that level. It is forbidden. What are you, some kind of moron? Get out of there before the Kaladan Agents see you. Are you deaf? I said you have to leave!" The one who was shouting threw something at him. It splattered on the walkway in a burst of pinkish-orange. It looked like some kind of fruit, but it smelled like roadkill. Sividious wrinkled his nose in disgust.

"I know you can understand me," the fruit-thrower said. "I can see the All Access Pass you are wearing. Now get out of here before the Secret Police arrive. I'm certain they are on their way by now. They have spies everywhere." He hefted another piece of fruit.

"I'm going! I'm going!" Sividious yelled, raising his hands to ward off the fruit. "Thanks for the warning."

The other shouted back, "This neighborhood simply can't afford any more trouble. Now scram!" He hurled the fruit, and it was all Sividious could do to avoid the sickening splatter. The horrible stench followed him into the alley as he ran.

Rats scattered at his approach, but he barely noticed, too intent on leaving this world to pay them any mind. As with the other worlds he had visited, the portal was not visible from this side, and he had to trust his sense of spacing to tell him when he was getting close. He was several paces from the back of the alley when the world flashed white around him and he found himself standing in the narrow passage of Portal Y16.

Alone in the quiet, he took a moment to consider what he had just learned. Y16 led to a world far more technologically advanced than Earth—a dazzling, magnificent world like those in his favorite sci-fi movies—and yet its citizens had shown an obvious fear of the Kaladan Agents. Even more important, they had known that what he wore around his neck was an AAP. That meant they knew about the stadium and its portals.

So did they participate in the Games? And if they did, were they willing participants or were they forced to compete like Aya?

He supposed it didn't really matter. What mattered was their warning about the Kaladan Agents. True, they had done it for selfish reasons, but it was clear they didn't think much of the fish-faced creatures. In fact, they seemed terrified of them.

All of it was important information, he decided. But it was information for later. Right now it might be best if he returned to Portal T16 so he could go home. He'd seen enough for one day. Truth be told, he'd seen enough to last him a lifetime.

He shook his head at the lie present in that last thought. *No*, he told himself, feeling a rush of excitement wash through him, *you have only just started.*

7
TIME DISCREPANCY

SIVIDIOUS WAS WITHIN SIGHT OF the portal to Earth when the lights of the stadium began to click on. Those in the main hallway came on first, chasing away all shadow as they glinted brightly off the burnished steel and smooth plastics. The lights in the portal hallways turned on next and were followed by the menu boards of the concession stands. A quick peek out through one of the concourses showed that banks of lights had risen from the top wall of the stadium and were beginning to come to life with a bright white glow.

The tower of box seats was already alight, and figures were visible moving within many of the levels. How they had arrived so quickly Sividious couldn't say, but it was clear the stadium was preparing for another round of the Games. The temptation to stay and watch was great, but Sividious knew he needed to leave before too many more patrons arrived. It was even more important to leave before any Agents appeared. They would certainly know T16 as a technologically primitive world and would question his possession of an AAP.

Quickening his step, he made for the portal as nonchalantly as he could, casually meeting the stares of a pair of green-skinned, lizard-looking creatures who were opening one of the concession stands. Fortunately, they only watched him for a moment before returning to their work. A pungent smell wafted from the stand as the gate came up, and Sividious held his breath as he walked by. Whatever passed for food on their particular planet smelled worse than the garbage cans in his school's cafeteria. He didn't even want to imagine what kind of being would deliberately eat something that smelled that bad.

As he neared Portal T16, he slowed, looking around to make sure no one was paying him any mind. When he was satisfied, he ducked into the narrow hallway and bolted for the portal.

He plunged through in a flash of white and was greeted by a blast of cool, damp air. In the near darkness, he tripped on the narrow strip of track and nearly pitched headlong onto his face.

In the distance ahead, the entrance of the mine was a bright square beckoning him onward, but he remained where he was for a few minutes and let his eyes adjust to the dimness surrounding him. When he could see the track at his feet, he took a deep breath of the cool, earth-scented air and carefully made his way out of the mine.

He stopped near the rusted mine car and looked around. Something wasn't right, he realized, but for a moment he couldn't decide what it was. Then he noticed the direction and length of his shadow stretching across the tailings, and his heart skipped a beat. Panicked, he squinted up at the sun to find it nearing the tops of the Wasatch Mountains. Its position confirmed his suspicion. It was late afternoon—he'd been gone for most of the day.

That isn't possible, he thought, frowning at his watch. It showed 8:35 A.M. He'd been inside the stadium for less than an hour. But even without his watch, he would have known he hadn't been gone for so long. He wasn't that bad at keeping track of time. He *knew* he had been in the stadium for only a short time.

He glanced at the afternoon shadows and shook his head. And yet he couldn't deny that it was afternoon. Apparently time moved differently in the stadium than it did on Earth. Obviously, Earth's time was much faster.

It's a good thing I didn't stay longer, he thought as he hurried for home. If he was late for dinner two nights in a row, his mother would ground him for a week.

He was making his way through the wilderness park when a sudden, horrifying thought stopped him in his tracks. What if it wasn't even the same day? What if . . . he hesitated. What if days had passed instead of hours?

He forced himself to start walking, but the thought of how much trouble he may have caused lay in his stomach like a sharp rock. If he had indeed been gone for days, an AMBER Alert would have been issued. Law enforcement and neighborhood volunteers would have been looking for him. He would have some serious explaining to do, and none of it could be about the stadium or its portals. Who would believe him anyway?

Leaving the wilderness park, he crossed the street to the mine museum and went in. Mr. Griffen, his curly gray hair in disarray, looked up from the book he was reading.

"Hello, Siv," he said, flashing a smile and pushing his thick glasses back up the bridge of his nose. He set the book down and moved out from behind the counter. "What brings you by today?"

Sividious took off his watch. "My watch stopped," he lied. "What time is it?"

Mr. Griffen squinted at his watch. "Four twenty," he answered.

Sividious nodded and began resetting his watch. "And today is the . . . ?"

"The eleventh," the older man said, and Sividious breathed a sigh of relief. It was still the same day.

He finished adjusting the time, then smiled at the aging museum owner. "Thanks," he said. "When your watch isn't working right, it's easy to lose track of time." *It's even easier when you're in a different galaxy,* he added silently. He started for the door. "Thanks again, Mr. Griffen."

Back outside, Sividious glanced up at the sun and shook his head in disbelief. Four twenty! Eight full hours later than what his watch had shown. It just didn't seem possible.

He started walking, and the mysteries of space and time weighed heavily on his mind. He supposed he should consider himself lucky. It could have been eight days instead of just eight hours. Now that he really thought about it, it could have been eight years!

He rubbed at his eyes. How would that be, he wondered, to leave for an hour and return to find that his little sister had become an adult, already graduated from high school, while he was still stuck in the eighth grade? Sam would have likely finished college and may even have gotten married. Heck, in eight years he might have even started a family.

And his mother . . . what would have become of her in eight years? What would losing a son have done to her? Would she have written him off as dead, or would she have held on to the hope that he would someday return? Would he have even been able to return after such a long time, especially since he wouldn't have aged more than an hour in eight long years?

Frowning, he took off the AAP and put it in his backpack. It might be a while before he used it again—if he decided to use it all. Losing eight hours of his life for every hour spent in the stadium didn't seem like a very good trade.

True, it was like a bizarre fountain of youth and could be used to slow his aging if he entered multiple times. He just didn't think he would enjoy having Simone be the same age. Or worse, older. With a trade of one hour for eight, she would eventually catch up to him.

The thought made him cringe. She was such a sassy-mouth now that he didn't even want to imagine what she might be like when she was fourteen.

Sighing heavily, he quickened his pace for home.

8
JACKIE

WHEN SIVIDIOUS ARRIVED HOME, HE found Jackie Molenshire sitting on the front porch waiting for him. His best friend since kindergarten, Jackie lived on a ranch just outside of Silver City, where her father was a top breeder of quarter horses. They also raised beef cattle and had hundreds of acres of land on which the animals could roam. Jackie had been in a saddle almost since she could walk and could probably ride better than. John Wayne. She absolutely loved animals and had more pets than the local zoo. After witnessing her prowess with animals, he wouldn't be at all surprised if she grew up to be a veterinarian or the owner of a wildlife preserve.

Right now, however, she looked more like John Wayne striding toward a shootout as she rose from the porch to meet him.

"Where have you been?" she asked as he turned through the front gate and started down the walk. Her dark brown eyes glimmered with concern, but her face was hard and angry. "When you didn't come to school today, I came to check on you, only to have Simone tell me that you went to the library to do research. But when I went to look for you there, no one had seen you all day. So then I came back here." She scowled at him. "My feet hurt from walking to and from the library, and I'm hungry, so you better have a darn good reason for disappearing for a whole day." She looked him up and down. "Kael didn't find you and beat the heck out of you, did he?"

"No," he answered, looking around to make sure Simone or Sam wasn't within earshot. "And could you keep it down? If Simone hears that I wasn't at the library, she'll tell my mom, and that would be worse than facing Kael."

"Fine," she said, her voice softer than before. "But you still have some explaining to do."

"Yes, I do," he said, looking into her eyes and knowing that he had already decided to tell her everything. He was glad there was still time before dinner. He had to tell someone about the stadium. It was too big a secret to keep locked away inside him. Perhaps talking about it would help him understand it better.

He took her by the arm and led her around the side of the house into the backyard. He sat in one of the swings on the swing set and motioned her to take the other.

When she was seated, he twisted his swing so he could meet her gaze. "Jackie, what I am about to tell you is so out there that you may not believe me. But you have to promise you will keep everything I tell you a secret."

"Well, duh," she said with a smile. "I've never told any of your other secrets, have I?"

"No," he admitted. "But those are nothing compared to this one. Those would only get me beat up or grounded. This one could get me killed."

Jackie's face sobered immediately. "Then you better tell me so I can help."

Sividious nodded then began his tale. He kept his voice low so only Jackie could hear, and he kept looking around nervously to make sure Simone wasn't trying to eavesdrop. He could tell by Jackie's face that she believed him, though he couldn't imagine how that was possible considering the fantastic nature of the tale.

He told her of Aya, of how he had met her and how she had given him the All Access Pass. He told her what Aya had said about the Games and how she had asked for help. He told of Aya's capture by the Kaladan Agents and their use of technologically superior weapons. He went into great detail about his trip through the portal to investigate the stadium and his travel to the three worlds he had visited, then he expressed his fear about the time discrepancy between this world and the stadium. He finished by showing her the All Access Pass and by telling her that he should probably never use it again.

"Are you kidding me?" she asked. "Of course you have to use it again. We have to help Aya."

Sividious stared at her. "You mean you believe me?"

"Well, of course," she said, her voice laced with that overly patient tone she always used whenever she felt he'd just asked a dumb question. "I am your best friend, after all."

"And this doesn't sound crazy to you?"

"I didn't say that," she answered. "It's completely crazy. But I've known you long enough to tell when you are lying, and this isn't one of those times."

Sividious felt the knot of anxiety inside him relax. He should have known Jackie would believe him. The only problem now would be trying to curb her enthusiasm about going to the stadium to see things for herself. Her eyes glimmered with that toss-caution-to-the-wind look that had gotten them both in trouble many times before.

"I can see what you are thinking," he told her. "And I'm telling you right now that we can't go back. The Kaladan Agents are too dangerous. If a world as technologically advanced as the one I visited is afraid of them, we should be too."

"We could get help," Jackie suggested.

"Help? From who?"

"The police. The military. Maybe the CIA or FBI."

Sividious raised an eyebrow at her. "Those are the last people we want to tell. Let's assume they believed us. Let's assume they wouldn't just toss us into a padded room at the funny farm and throw away the key. They would certainly take the AAP for themselves, classify the investigation, and restrict us from ever entering the stadium again. Then, like they always do, they would overreact in some hostile, shoot-first-ask-questions-later militaristic way and get our world destroyed by the Kaladan."

"You watch too many science fiction movies," Jackie said.

"Yeah, well, there is truth in stereotypes. Involving the military would be a disaster. As advanced as our civilization is, we aren't much more than cavemen compared to the technology of many of those other worlds. And the simple fact that the Kaladan Agents are some sort of secret police with access to every one of those worlds suggests they are *the* force to be reckoned with. After what I saw of their technology, they would squash our military like so many pesky bugs."

"So it's up to us," Jackie told him.

"To do what?"

She gave him a patient stare before answering. "To help Aya. We have to, Siv. You said yourself that there is only us. She needs us."

Sividious rubbed his eyes wearily. He should have known Jackie would want to help. She was forever taking in and caring for stray animals, nursing them to health and finding homes for those her father wouldn't let her keep —like the black bear cub of last year and the baby mountain lion from the year before. It was part of the reason he thought she might someday own a wildlife refuge.

But Aya was not a lost or injured animal. She was a creature from another world. One who found herself on the wrong side of a powerful and dangerous organization. An organization that could easily enslave or destroy every living thing on Earth.

And that, he realized suddenly, was exactly the reason he and Jackie needed to help the young Kelsprite. In all the myriad galaxies he'd seen in the night sky of the stadium, there were only two people who knew or cared about her plight. And he did care, he decided. He cared enough to risk going back into the stadium.

"Okay," he told Jackie. "We'll help." When she smiled, he made a cautionary motion with his hand. "But we will need to really think this through before we do. If there's such a huge discrepancy between time here and time in the stadium, we'll need to move quickly. Every fifteen minutes there is two stinking hours here."

"We'll need to do it during a time when we won't be missed," Jackie added. "Like after school or on a Saturday or something."

"Right," he agreed then pursed his lips worriedly. "But we are going to have to be really careful. We don't want anyone to see us going up to the mine. Especially somebody like Kael. The rumors he could spread about something like that . . . we'd never live it down."

"I've about had it with Kael," Jackie muttered darkly. "That guy really needs an attitude adjustment."

Sividious snorted. "Well, it's not going to be by me."

Jackie ignored the comment. "Kael isn't the only one who might blab about us going into the wilderness park together. People always assume the worst. And you have to admit that two teenagers going into the wilderness park alone might give people the wrong idea. It would probably be best if we went in at different times and in different places. We could meet at the entrance to the mine."

Sividious was quiet a minute as he considered. As important as all these things were, he and Jackie hadn't addressed any of the real dangers associated with this venture—those involving the loss of life and limb. Or worse, the loss of freedom. He looked into Jackie's dark brown eyes then leaned forward for emphasis.

"The rumors people might spread about us will be the least of our worries if we are caught by the Kaladan," he told her. "If they don't just kill us outright, they will surely throw us into the Games, which might have the same result anyway. Aya was fearful that she wouldn't last another week. Either way, we won't be coming back to Earth. Our families will never know the truth behind our disappearance."

"We could leave a will of sorts," Jackie suggested. "A letter explaining where we went and what happened to us."

Sividious raised an eyebrow at her. "And be remembered as a couple of crackpot kids who ran away from home," he told her. "No, thank you." He shook his head. "If we are going to do this—and I want to go on record that we are crazy to even try—it needs to be kept between us. No one else can know."

Jackie took a deep breath and slowly let it out before nodding. "Okay," she said, smiling nervously. "So, when do we go?"

"Tomorrow, right after school," Sividious answered. "If we ride the bus as far as the library, we can walk the rest of the way to the wilderness park, splitting up before we head out. We'll have two hours or so where we won't be missed."

They talked of other things for a while: homework, the science project that was coming up, Kael and his band of thugs—small talk designed to take their minds off tomorrow. None of it worked, of course; the prospect of entering the stadium was simply too exciting to ignore for long.

"What should we take with us?" Jackie asked after a particularly long silence.

Sividious jumped in spite of himself. He'd just been thinking the same thing. "I don't know," he said. "I don't think we need to take much food, because we won't be in there for very long. And I don't think we should take any kind of a weapon. It might tick off the wrong people if we get caught. We don't want the Kaladan thinking the Earth was staging a coup or launching an invasion."

"With two teenagers?" Jackie asked incredulously. "Come on, Siv. How threatening do you think we would be to a technologically superior race?"

"Who knows." Sividious told her. "But after seeing how they treated Aya, it might be best not to find out."

They fell silent again, each lost in thought as they contemplated the next day. It was Jackie who finally broke the silence.

"I probably ought to get home before my parents start to worry about me," she told him, rising from the swing and stretching her back.

"How are you getting home?"

"On your bike, of course. You didn't think I was going to walk all that way, did you? Especially with all the walking I did trying to find you. I'll ride back in the morning, and then we can ride the bus together."

Sividious ran to get his bike then walked Jackie out to the sidewalk. "I'll see you in the morning," he told her as she climbed on. "Bring whatever you think we might need, and I'll do the same."

She said she would, and Sividious watched her until she was out of sight. He was glad Jackie believed him about the stadium. He was even more glad she was his friend. Without her encouragement, he might have been enough of a coward to forget the whole thing.

Turning up the walk, he sighed deeply when he realized how tired he was. He may have skipped eight whole hours today, but it sure didn't feel like it. A lousy night's sleep and the stress of exploring the stadium had left him feeling like he'd been awake for a week. He hoped tomorrow would be better, but he couldn't shake the feeling that his life was about to plunge headlong into chaos.

9
A SUDDEN ABSENCE OF COOTIES

THE NEXT MORNING, SIVIDIOUS WOKE long before his alarm sounded, but instead of trying to return to sleep, he rose and made ready for the day. He'd slept well in spite of his nervousness, a result, perhaps, of being so tired.

He dressed quickly, then turned his attention to his backpack. What to take? he wondered. What would be most valuable on a trip into the stadium? He packed the AAP—there would be no trip without it—and tossed in a few granola bars and a bag of beef jerky. He rifled through his dresser drawers until he found the stopwatches his dad had given him last Christmas then clicked a few buttons to make sure they worked. Satisfied, he tucked them in his pack as well.

Not sure what else to bring, he slung his pack over his shoulder and went to the kitchen to get breakfast. His mom was there, packing a lunch for Simone.

"Feeling better today?" his mother asked.

"Much better," he told her. "So much so that I probably ought to stay after school so I can get caught up on my homework."

His mother said she thought that was a good idea then went to her room to finish getting ready for work. Sividious hurriedly downed a bowl of cereal before heading out front to wait for Jackie. He didn't have to wait long. She arrived on his bike a few minutes later with a large duffle bag hanging from one shoulder.

"What's in there?" he asked as she set the bag on the ground in front of him. Two long shafts tipped in red protruded from the zippered end.

"Stuff we might need," she answered, sounding proud of herself.

Sividious unzipped the bag and peered inside. Each red-tipped shaft ended at a green handle shaped like a pistol grip. He looked up at Jackie.

"Are those what I think they are?" he asked.

She nodded. "HS36 Cattle Prods. Nine thousand volts of pure shock. And trust me. You don't want to be on the receiving end of those babies unless you have a hide as thick as a cow."

"Uh . . . okay," he said, still not sure it was a good idea to carry anything weapon-like with them and somewhat skeptical as to why they would need cattle prods in the stadium anyway. He dug deeper in the bag and found an assortment of snacks—at least he and Jackie were on the same page there—a tube of lipstick, and two karate uniforms.

"What are the karate uniforms for?" he asked.

"So we won't look like we are from Earth," she explained patiently. "Jeans and T-shirts are so . . . so . . . well, earthly. The karate uniforms are more exotic looking. Besides, I fight better when I'm in my uniform. It puts me in my zone."

Sividious smiled. As stupid as it sounded, he thought she might be right. The uniforms were simple, but they weren't as common as jeans and T-shirts. And they might be just ethnic enough to pass them off as people from a world other than Earth. Unless the Kaladan Agents were familiar with Asian culture, he thought, in which case it wouldn't matter. On a brighter note, Jackie was a black belt, and if she felt more comfortable in her uniform than in jeans, who was he to argue? She had won the gold medal for karate for her age division during the Utah Summer Games last year and had thumped on people almost twice her size to win it.

He held up the lipstick. "And this?" he asked, giving her an odd look.

"That's pepper spray," she said. "My mom carries it in her purse. The lipstick case is a disguise."

"Oh," he said, then zipped the bag shut and stood. "You know we can't take this stuff to school, right? If we were caught with it, we would get expelled."

"I know," she said. "I thought we could leave it here. Instead of getting off at the library, we can ride the bus home after school and get it before going to the wilderness park."

They put the bag in the storage shed in the backyard then went out to the bus stop to wait for the bus. They were joined by some of their classmates, and Sividious quickly became the center of attention.

"We missed you at school yesterday, Siv," Brayden Peterson said as he joined them. "Were you sick?"

"Sick of Kael," Sividious replied.

Alexis Sheffield laughed, but her face sobered almost immediately. "He was looking for you yesterday," she told him. "He said he is going to beat the crap out of you for what you did to him."

"I didn't do anything to him," Sividious said, trying for his best tone of innocence. "Kael just can't handle Mexican food and probably shouldn't have eaten a second helping of refried beans during lunch that day."

Alexis stared at him skeptically. "I don't think all the beans in the lunchroom could have made him sound like that," she said.

Sividious shrugged, turning to Brayden. "Did we get any homework in biology?"

"Nothing that you won't be able to do in five minutes," Brayden answered, sounding jealous. He looked at Jackie. "So, how come you're riding the bus with us today?" he asked. He tried to keep his voice neutral, but his excitement was visible anyway. It was no secret that he liked Jackie. Some might even call it a crush.

Unfortunately for Brayden, Jackie didn't share the sentiment. In fact, she was so irritated by his interest in her that she went out of her way to tease, taunt, and insult him every chance she got. Sividious could tell by the look in her eyes that now would be no different.

She smiled sweetly. "Well, I was over at Siv's last night until so late that it was easier to spend the night than it was to go home."

Brayden's face darkened, but he said nothing. Alexis, on the other hand, began to giggle. So did Sarah and Michelle Hollister. The twins put their heads together to exchange whispers then glanced at Brayden and started laughing again.

Shooting Jackie a warning look, Sividious came to Brayden's rescue. "Jackie borrowed my bike yesterday," he told them. "She rode to my house this morning to return it. She hasn't spent the night at my house since we were six years old."

He realized by the frown still creasing Brayden's face that the boy wasn't comforted. Apparently, he was jealous about Jackie having *ever* spent the night at Sividious's house. Lucky for Brayden, the bus arrived before any of the girls could resume their teasing.

Jackie and Sividious took a seat near the back of the bus, away from the others. They waited until the bus was underway so the roar of the engine would drown out anything the friends might say.

"You should really lay off of Brayden," Sividious said quietly. "I'm sure he means well."

"I don't like the way he looks at me," Jackie grumbled. "It creeps me out."

"It's not his fault you're so good-looking," Sividious told her then realized what he had said and looked away, his face burning with embarrassment.

Jackie elbowed him in the ribs to make him look at her. Her face was a mixture of curiosity and amusement, but there was something else in her eyes that sent a strange tickle through Sividious's chest. "Do *you* think I'm good-looking?" she asked.

Sividious swallowed hard. "You're my best friend, aren't you?"

She leaned close and looked him directly in the eyes. "You didn't answer the question," she told him.

Sividious met her gaze levelly, but his stomach began doing somersaults. "I think you are the prettiest girl in the whole school," he said softly. "And I'm not saying that just because you're my best friend either." He shot a quick look to see if anyone was watching and found Brayden peering at them from over the back of his seat a few rows away. Sividious returned his gaze to Jackie. "I'm saying it because it's true."

Jackie leaned back against the seat, a satisfied look on her face. "You realize, of course, that this conversation is taking place five years later than it should have," she said. "Girls like to be told they are pretty, Siv. Even when they are your best friend. *Especially* when they are."

Sividious stared at her, silently relieved by her reaction. He'd been worried that she might react to him the way she had to Brayden. He was also relieved that he had finally been able to say what he'd been thinking since the day they'd first met in kindergarten. Still, he couldn't let her off that easy.

He grinned at her. "I didn't say anything five years ago because you still had cooties," he told her.

"And now?" she asked, her eyes narrowing dangerously.

He reached up and picked through her hair the way a mother chimp might groom its baby. "Nope. Looks like they are all gone."

"I'm so glad," she said dryly and slugged him in the side so hard it hurt.

They laughed for a moment then fell silent, each left to wrestle with their own thoughts. Sividious stared out the window as they rode, pretending to study the wilderness park and its surroundings. Really, it was to keep from looking at Jackie. He could feel her eyes on him, but he refused to meet her gaze.

He was startled by the sudden turn of events, and he was still trying to come to terms with how their relationship may have just changed. Jackie was his best friend, and he loved her dearly. But that love had always been the pure, un-messed-up-by-hormones-or-romantic-feelings love of friendship. He wasn't sure he wanted that to change.

As if sensing his thoughts, Jackie leaned close and spoke softly into his ear. "It's okay that the cooties are gone, Siv. I would worry about you if you didn't think I was pretty. I might even be insulted by it." She flashed a grin and elbowed him in the ribs. "But if you start to treat me any differently, I might have to kill you. We can worry about the future when we're old enough to drive."

"Sounds like a plan," he told her, relief washing through him. "But first we have to make it through the rest of today."

10
RETURN TO THE STADIUM

THINKING BACK ON HIS COMMENT about making it through the rest of today, Sividious realized he'd been referring to surviving a trip into the stadium. It never occurred to him that he would have to survive school first. The oversight came to light the moment he stepped off the bus.

"There you are, you little jerk," Kael said as he moved to block Sividious's way. His face was hard, his hands balled into fists. "It's time I kicked your trash."

Before Sividious could answer, Jackie stepped in front of him to face Kael. "Maybe it's time I kicked yours," she told him. Her stance was relaxed, but her voice was so menacing that Kael took an unconscious step backward.

He recovered quickly, his lips curling into a frown. "You even think about using that karate crap on me," Kael snarled, "and I'll—"

Jackie moved so fast that Kael was flat on his back and gasping for air before those looking on even realized she had moved. She put her foot on his throat and pressed down hard enough to make his eyes bulge. "Listen to me, you oversized ape," she said, looking down at him the way an exterminator might look at a cockroach in need of squishing. "Sividious is my friend. You threaten him and you are threatening me. So unless you want to find out what I am really capable of with my *karate crap,* you will stay away from him." She eyed Kael's cronies with contempt. "That goes for the rest of you morons too."

"Okay, that's enough," an adult voice said, and they all turned to see Mrs. Hadley, the bus driver, stepping from the bus. "Jacolyn, please let Kael up. The rest of you get along to class." She waited until she was obeyed then turned to Kael, who was rubbing his throat. "Are you all right, Kael?" she asked.

"I'm fine," he grumbled, scowling at Jackie. He turned his gaze on Sividious. "But you won't be when I catch you without your girlfriend to protect you. You're a dead man, Stark." He turned and stalked away, and his group of thugs hurried to join him.

Mrs. Hadley smiled at Jackie. "You realize, of course, that I only stopped you because my job requires it of me. Personally, I would have liked to watch you thrash him." She winked at Jackie and climbed back into the bus.

"Thanks," Sividious whispered to Jackie as they started for the school.

"You're welcome," she said, then sighed. "I just hope you don't get teased too much because a girl had to save you."

Sividious shrugged. "It couldn't possibly be as painful as what would have happened otherwise." He laughed. "Besides, if anyone is going to get teased, it'll be Kael. He's the one who embarrassed himself in front of his friends."

* * *

The rest of the school day was uneventful, and time passed far too slowly for Sividious's liking. It was difficult to keep his mind on his schoolwork, and he found himself daydreaming about the stadium more times than he would have liked. When the last bell finally rang, he nearly shouted for joy.

Out in the hallway, he found Jackie closing her locker. When she spotted him, she asked, "You ready for this?"

"I've been ready all day," he answered. "Come on, let's get to the bus before Kael comes looking for me."

"He won't," Jackie said, sounding extremely satisfied.

Sividious arched an eyebrow at her. "What did you do?"

"I dropped him on his back again after he made a couple of derogatory comments about my friendship with you."

"And you didn't get in trouble?"

"Nope. It was during PE, and Mr. Bernhard wasn't watching." She gave an evil laugh. "Kael might be big, but he's slower than a dead cow and just about as smart as one."

They rode the bus to Sividious's house to get their bag of supplies then walked separately to the wilderness park. When they were together again, they started the climb up to the mine. As they picked their way through the tangled oak brush, they made their plan for entering the stadium. They would each carry a cattle prod, and Sividious would carry the backpack of snacks. Their *earthly* clothes would be stashed in Jackie's duffle bag and left in the mine. The pepper spray tube and Jackie's snacks would be transferred to Sividious's pack. They would take a quick look around the stadium—no more than fifteen minutes—before returning to Earth to discuss further options. *What could go wrong?* Sividious thought then frowned inwardly. *Besides everything, of course.*

Each took a turn changing into a karate uniform inside the mine while the other waited outside. When they finished, Sividious put the AAP around his neck then took out both of his stopwatches and clicked them on. One he placed in his backpack, the other he set on top of the duffle bag holding their clothes. "That way," he told Jackie, "we'l know exactly how long we were in the stadium."

Hefting his cattle prod in front of him, he took Jackie by the hand. "I suspect we both have to be touching for the AAP to work," he explained. "Hold on tight. The first time is a bit of a rush."

The light around them grew dim as they moved deeper into the mine, and the air turned cool. Sividious tightened his hold on Jackie's hand. "We're almost there," he whispered and felt her body tense. A heartbeat later the world flashed white around them.

They were standing inside the shiny metal and plastic corridor of Portal T16.

"Wow," Jackie said softly. Her eyes were wide with wonder as she took in her surroundings. She gestured to the odd-looking letters above the shimmering wall of the portal. "What does that say?"

Sividious removed the AAP and put it around Jackie's neck. "Read it for yourself," he told her.

"Portal T16," she said then turned to look at him, the excitement evident in her eyes as she fingered the AAP. "This is awesome." She started to remove the AAP to give it back, but Sividious waved her off.

"Keep it on," he told her. "I've been here before, so I kind of know my way around. On this level at least. If we go anywhere else, I'll need you to translate."

Still holding hands, they made their way to the larger, inner corridor and peeked around the corner. The place was dark save for a smattering of security lights and the soft green glow of what appeared to be a sweeper robot's headlights as it made its way down the corridor, its rotating brush filling the stillness with a stiff, whisking sound. The concession stands were closed. Night held sway beyond the concourse openings.

"The portals are in alphabetical order," he told her once the sweeper robot disappeared around the bend. "I think the number indicates the level. The portal to Earth is on Level 16."

"And the worlds you visited," Jackie said, "they were on this level also?"

"Yes," Sividious said with a nod. "I didn't have time to visit any of the other levels. I'm not even sure how many there are, but from what I saw when I peeked outside, it didn't look like the stadium concourses went higher than twenty or so."

He pointed to the entrance of the nearest concourse. "Come on," he said. "You've got to see the night sky above this place. It's amazing."

They moved out into the stadium, and Jackie gasped at the backdrop of stars and galaxies. "That is the most beautiful thing I've ever seen," she whispered. "It looks like you could reach up and touch them, doesn't it?"

"Some of them you can," he told her, "by going through a portal."

Jackie shivered. "It makes me feel so small and insignificant."

"Me too," Sividious said. "But it's also kind of exciting." He turned to look at her. "Where would you like to go next?"

"Up," she said, "I want to see what's over the top edge."

Sividious grinned at her. "That's why I like you," he told her. "You think like I do. Come on. I know where an elevator is."

"Forget the elevator," Jackie said. "We can take the stairs up through the bleachers." She looked up at the galaxies turning slowly overhead. "It will be like we're climbing through space."

"I don't think that's far from the truth," he told her as they started up the stairs.

When they reached the top—Level 20, if Sividious had counted correctly—they stood on the last row of bleachers and peered over the wall at what lay beyond the stadium. What they found gave Sividious a sudden feeling of vertigo, and he gripped the top of the wall to steady himself.

As he had suspected, there was nothing beyond the stadium but the never-ending vastness of space. Stars and galaxies of all shapes and colors stretched away into infinity. And the stadium—he swallowed hard—the stadium seemed to be floating in the middle of it all, like an iceberg in dark waters.

Jackie's voice trembled with fear as she spoke. "Where is this place?"

Sividious shrugged. "In between."

"In between what?"

"Everything."

Jackie pointed down. "Look how it's shaped," she said. "It flares out like an iceberg. And the top levels, which I guess are the bleachers for the stadium, are only half the size of the levels below. This place is massive."

Sividious had already come to the same conclusion. Even more importantly, he noticed how each of the lower levels had narrow corridors extending from the main body of the stadium just like the top half did. They stuck out like the bristles of a brush or the quills of a giant porcupine.

"More portals," he said aloud. "And they're much bigger than the one we just used."

"I wonder what they are for."

"We'll have to come back later to figure that out," he told her. He pulled the stopwatch from his backpack and showed her the time. "We've been here for almost fifteen minutes. Two hours will have passed back home."

As they made their way back down the stairs of the bleachers, Sividious noticed that the lights in some of the box seats in the tower had come on. Shapes were visible moving inside.

"I think the Games are about to begin again," he told Jackie, pointing to the tower. "We should probably hurry."

They picked up the pace, striding down the stairs two and three at a time. Below them, the black hole that was the playing field gradually grew visible as banks of overhead lights began clicking on. By the time they reached Level 16, the stadium had turned bright as day. The stars and galaxies were still visible, but their brilliance was muted by the glow filling the stadium.

Pausing at the entrance to their concourse, Sividious studied the playing field below. An oval expanse of green about the size of a football field, it was surrounded by a wall some twenty feet high. Passages of various sizes and shapes opened onto the playing field, depthless holes that stretched into the bowels of the stadium, dark and uninviting.

"That must be where the players come from," Jackie said, indicating the array of dark passages. "That's where we will find Aya."

"If she's still here," Sividious said, but what he really meant and couldn't bring himself to say was, *If she's still alive.*

He studied the different levels of seats for a moment and realized that about half of the levels catered to beings other than humanoids—the seats and benches were too oddly shaped for people. Six levels below them, the concourse had no seats at all, just an expanse of smooth metal on the same grade as the stairs rising through it. After a moment of wondering about what might sit—or float—there, he finally nudged Jackie. "Come on, let's get out of here."

Back in the narrow corridor of Portal T16, they held hands as they stepped through the shimmering, liquid-like surface of the portal and returned to Earth.

11
QUESTIONS OF TIME

SIVIDIOUS WAITED FOR HIS EYES to adjust to the near darkness of the mine then tucked the cattle prod under his arm and moved to the stopwatch he'd left on the duffle bag. It read four minutes and forty-eight seconds.

"That can't be right," he said, checking it against the one he had taken with him. "This watch shows we were inside for fifteen minutes but this one has yet to reach five."

"Let me see," Jackie said then frowned thoughtfully. After a moment, she said, "Maybe the stadium isn't just a place between worlds, maybe it's in between times, too."

"But last time I went in, eight hours passed," Sividious told her. "And I was only gone an hour."

"But last time you went through three portals. Maybe that's what created the time difference."

Sividious thought about it, his mind racing over what he knew about Einstein's theory of relativity. There was a lot to it, of course, but to put it simply, the faster an object traveled through space, the slower time passed for that object.

"I'll bet you're right," he said at last. "If any one of the worlds I went to was moving faster than Earth does, time would have slowed for me there, while time here would have continued on its merry, speedier way."

Jackie stared at him. "Uh . . . what?"

"It's Einstein's theory of relativity," he told her excitedly. "Einstein believed—"

"I'll take your word for it," Jackie said, cutting him off. She looked at the stopwatches. "So how do you explain the difference this time?"

Sividious shrugged. "I can't," he told her. "But don't you see what this means?" he asked excitedly. "It means as long as we don't leave the stadium, we can stay there for long stretches of time. Time moves slower here than it does there. Three times slower, apparently."

He reset both watches to zero and handed one to Jackie. "Here, I'll prove it to you. I'll go back into the stadium. You click the stopwatch as soon as I enter, then click it again when I return. I'll click mine once I'm through the portal, then I'll wait a full fifteen minutes. If I'm right, I'll be gone no more than five minutes of your time."

Jackie looked skeptical, but she agreed. She handed him the All Access Pass then put her thumb on the button of the stopwatch. "Whenever you're ready," she told him.

Hanging the AAP around his neck, Sividious tightened his grip on the cattle prod and stepped through the portal in a humming flash of white. As soon as he was on the other side, he clicked the stopwatch and moved down the narrow passage toward the main corridor. The lights had come on in the few Earth minutes he had been away, and "people" were starting to arrive from their respective worlds. Those who weren't lining up at the concession stands were moving through to the bleachers.

Sividious stayed in the relative safety of the smaller portal passage and watched as beings of every shape, color, and size streamed by. Most looked like they had walked out of the pages of a sci-fi pulp magazine, bizarre creatures, more animal than human.

One group, slender bird-like creatures with large, luminous eyes and wings of grayish leather, moved by in a rapid bobbing gate, their three-toed claws clacking loudly on the floor. Another group of multilegged monstrosities lumbered by in a blur of appendages and bluish fur. Three sets of red eyes peered out from the bulbous mounds of their faces.

Sividious watched them pass then turned his attention to a cluster of small, insect-looking folk who were skittering up to the concession stand. They weren't much larger than cats, but every creature around them took note of their presence and kept a healthy distance. Behind them, five yellow-and-orange ape things floated high above the floor on what looked like silver hubcaps. Their diminutive size and the floating contraptions reminded Sividious of the floating chair Yoda used in *Attack of the Clones*.

And yet there were a fair number of humanoids as well, some of whom would have blended in with any of Earth's populations just fine. Most, however, would have only blended in at a rock concert or a bizarre fashion show in Paris. Some looked like they were on their way to starring in a Shakespeare play. A few looked like they were on their way to a Halloween party.

And there were weapons. Lots of them. Most looked to be technological—guns and bombs and energy wands like the Kaladan Agents had carried—but there were also a lot of swords and shields and bows and knives. Some of the more alien creatures weren't much more than walking weapons themselves. And every creature, both alien and humanoid alike, watched every other creature warily. Suspicion and distrust filled the air like a heavy mist.

Many of those Sividious surveyed wore lanyards similar to the one he had on, but the passes themselves were different. They were smaller and made of a different color of plastic than the All Access Pass that Aya had stolen from the Kaladan Agents. He couldn't say for sure, but he suspected the smaller passes only allowed access to whatever world the wearer was from. It made him think he should keep his own pass hidden since it was likely that the only people who had an AAP were the Kaladan and those who worked for them. Anyone else wearing one would certainly draw the wrong kind of attention. He quickly tucked the AAP inside his karate uniform.

With some difficulty, he shook himself free of the spectacle in front of him and looked at the stopwatch. Fourteen minutes and counting. It was time to get back to Jackie.

Turning his back on the parade of weirdness, Sividious walked to the portal and stepped through.

He found Jackie where he had left her, facing the portal, stopwatch gripped in her hand. She clicked the button with her thumb the moment he appeared, but her eyes were doubtful as she looked at the time.

"Five minutes thirteen seconds," she said.

Sividious showed her his stopwatch. It showed fifteen minutes and counting. "I was right," he said. "Time moves slower here than it does inside the stadium." He took the stopwatch from her and laid it on the duffle bag. "But," he added, "we'll leave this running anyway. We need to keep track of time in case we enter any of the other portals. Obviously, the space-time relationship between other worlds and the stadium is different than our own. I want to know how long I am gone."

She arched an eyebrow at him. "We're going back in?" she asked. "I thought we left because the Games were starting and we didn't want anyone to see us."

"Yeah, well, I don't think it will be a problem anymore," he said. "There are beings and creatures from hundreds of worlds in there right now. I doubt anyone will notice us at all."

He paused, motioning to her cattle prod. "But bring that just in case," he said. "Some of the creatures I saw looked a bit on the unfriendly side. We don't want them thinking we will be easy victims."

"Sividious," she said, her voice wary, "what aren't you telling me?"

"A lot," he answered then flashed a reassuring smile. "But it's stuff you have to see for yourself. It is absolutely amazing."

Jackie studied him without speaking, her eyes narrow as she nervously bit her lip. Finally, she nodded and bent to retrieve the cattle prod. "I hope you're right about this," she said, taking him by the hand. "Because my built-in danger-o-meter just went off the charts."

"Your what?"

"Call it woman's intuition," she answered. "It's a little something girls have that keeps them from doing stupid things."

"You think this is stupid?"

"It has been from the start."

"And . . . ?" he asked.

She grinned at him. "I wouldn't miss it for the world."

12
BLACK BELTS AND CATTLE PRODS

Back inside the stadium, Jackie and Sividious held hands as they moved into the main corridor and joined the throng of alien creatures making their way to their seats. Jackie surveyed the vast array of clothing styles and smiled. She'd been right about the karate uniforms blending in—no one even gave them a second glance. Even the Hot-Shot cattle prods she and Sividious carried barely drew any attention.

But that, she decided, was a bit worrisome. It either meant that weapons were so commonplace here that they were taken for granted, or it meant a cattle prod wasn't very threatening. Neither option was comforting.

"I think we might be a little overmatched in the weapons department," she whispered, indicating the assault rifle strapped to the back of a large, furry creature who resembled Bigfoot.

"Maybe," Sividious said. "But for all we know, Mr. Sasquatch there is thinking the same thing about the cattle prods." He turned and looked at her, his face still bright with excitement for the wonder of the place. "If the weapons the Kaladan Agents used on Aya are any indication, the more dangerous a weapon looks, the less dangerous it really is."

She raised an eyebrow at him.

"Don't you see?" he asked. "Those sticks of theirs had a very simple design but packed one heck of a punch." He nodded toward a group of scaled humanoids watching them from a concession stand. "See those guys over there?" he asked. "The lizard-looking ones. They have been discussing the cattle prods since the moment they first saw us. Apparently, they look like a weapon used by a rogue military group on their homeworld. And the karate uniforms," he added, "have quite a reputation as well."

"How do you know that?"

He tapped the AAP tucked beneath his uniform. "I have this, remember?"

"Oh, right," she said, troubled that the uniforms might be doing the opposite of what she intended. In fact, now that she was aware of it, she noticed how most of the creatures looked the other way when they saw her and Sividious. And it wasn't because the uniforms were commonplace; it was obvious they were scaring people. Frowning, she changed the subject. "So where are we going?"

"To see what these Games are all about," he answered. "I'm sure there will be empty seats somewhere. If not, we'll watch from the entrance of one of the concourses." He angled toward what looked like an elevator. "But I think I would like to get a little closer to the playing field."

When they reached the burnished silver doors, Sividious pushed the down button, and they waited quietly for the elevator to move to their level. Something large and white moved to stand next to them, but before Jackie could take a closer look, the door opened and she and Sividious moved inside. The large alien moved in beside them and pushed a button near the bottom.

Sividious scanned the rows of buttons briefly before pushing one near the middle. "Stadium Level 3," he told her then pointed to the rows of buttons below the midway point. "That character there, the one that looks like an upside-down *V* with a line over it is the symbol for under. Those are the sublevels of this place—the big part we saw when we looked over the edge. Our companion here is headed for Sublevel 12."

Jackie nodded, then turned to study the odd-looking being standing beside her. It had the face of a pig, with large tusks and tiny pink eyes, but its body was hairless and smooth. It wore a simple red loincloth around its waist and a beaded necklace with a plastic ID badge around its neck. Its limbs were thick, bulbous protrusions that made it look like a cross between a sumo wrestler and a giant radish.

It noticed her stare and turned to look at her, its tiny pink eyes sparkling with amusement. "*Jemkalat to yorowasi sel poto?*" it said, and Jackie turned to Sividious for help.

"He said, 'Have you never seen a Jemkalat before, young one?'" Sividious told her.

She shook her head. "No," she answered and dipped her head in apology. "Tell him I'm sorry for staring," she told Sividious.

"You just did," Sividious said. "His Access Pass is similar to mine and allows him to understand any language."

The Jemkalat nodded, and his pig face broke into a large smile, revealing two rows of pearly-white teeth. He looked like he was about to say more, but the elevator beeped and the doors opened to Level 3.

Bidding the Jemkalat farewell, Sividious took Jackie by the hand and led her out into the throng of spectators making their way into the bleachers. "Let's see if there is a place to sit," Sividious said, and they moved out into the vastness of the stadium arena.

As the concourse walls fell away and the arena came into view, it was all Jackie could do to keep herself from gasping out loud. Hundreds of thousands of beings filled the bleachers, hundreds of thousands of *different* kinds of beings from innumerable worlds.

"Right there on the aisle," Sividious said, pointing to seats a couple of rows down. "If the ticket holders show up, we'll move."

"Ticket holders?" Jackie asked.

"You didn't think all of this was free, did you?" he said. He pointed at a group of feathered humanoids looking at shiny silver ticket stubs as they moved down a row, checking the numbers on their tickets against the numbers on the seats. "Those who don't have Access Passes have to purchase tickets. I've heard several of the patrons complaining about how the Kaladan raised the price again."

"I need to get me an AAP," Jackie said, "so I can hear what is going on around this place."

"I'm sorry," Sividious said, reaching for the lanyard. "Here, wear this one."

Jackie put a hand on his arm to stop him. "On second thought," she said, eyeing a cluster of snake-headed creatures who were hissing at a tall humanoid who'd taken a seat in front of them, "I don't think I want to hear what some of these things are saying."

Sividious grunted as if he thought that might be best then led her to two empty seats next to the aisle. When they were seated, Jackie looked around in awe. She couldn't believe how big the place was or how many seats the stadium had. It had to be close to a million. The drone of voices from the spectators was deafening.

Suddenly a loud hum filled the stadium, a pulsating sound that moved from high to low as if someone were trying to tune a radio to the proper channel. As the hum faded, the myriad of languages being spoken around Jackie became one language, and she understood every word.

"Take off the AAP," she whispered and watched as Sividious lifted the lanyard from around his neck.

"Cool," he said. "I wondered how they were going to communicate with those who don't have one of these. But it makes sense that if they can do it on an individual level for those who have an AAP, they can do it during the Games."

The gigantic television screens towering above each end zone flared to life, and Jackie and Sividious watched with fascination as products from a dozen worlds were advertised for sale at the concession stands. At the end of the commercials, the face of a woman appeared. Her skin was the most beautiful hue of purple Jackie had ever seen, and her eyes were a brilliant green. Her hair was jet black, and when she smiled, her teeth were as white as snow. Despite the odd coloration, she was the most beautiful woman Jackie had ever seen. The spectators must have thought so as well, because the drone of voices in the stadium fell to near silence.

"Welcome, citizens of the universe, to today's Games," the woman said cheerily. "Today, in addition to five matches for the Sproark Invitational, you will witness a semifinal round for the Jomon Worlds of Magic Tournament. Today's Jomon contest features Aya the Kelsprite from the world of Fallisor in the Promor Galaxy."

Jackie stiffened in surprise and turned to find Sividious looking equally stunned. Around them the crowd cheered wildly, and a rhythmic chant sprang up.

"Aya! Aya! Aya!"

Jackie shook her head in disbelief. Apparently the young Kelsprite was a crowd favorite.

In contrast, the crowd booed loudly as her opponent was named. "Aya will face Shoar the Dragon Centipede from Osotepu, also from the Promor Galaxy."

"What the heck is a Dragon Centipede?" Sividious asked, and Jackie shrugged.

Behind them a green-and-yellow humanoid with two sets of arms and large luminous eyes provided the answer. "A Dragon Centipede," he said, drawing their eyes to his, "is a creature of dark magic, ancient of date, with a very nasty temperament. Aya, bless her little blue heart, won't last two minutes against the cursed thing." He—at least Jackie thought it was a he—shook his head sadly. "Word has it the Kaladan Agents recruited the Dragon Centipede to eliminate Aya from the competition because she angered one of their chieftains. She was supposed to face a Buzz Crawler from the world of Mord, but it died in a 'freak accident' on its way to the Locker Rooms."

The green-and-yellow face twisted into a frown. "She would have had an easy time with the Buzz Crawler. Now . . ." He trailed off meaningfully.

"When is Aya's match?" Sividious asked.

"After the invitational," the other answered. "The Kaladan like to build toward a climax."

"Then we have some time," Sividious muttered aloud. Jackie frowned a warning at him as the green-and-yellow creature leaned forward questioningly.

"Time? Time to do what?" he asked.

"To get something to eat," she answered. "Come on, Siv. Let's head back to the concession stands."

They started to rise, but two large shapes were blocking their way. "What are you vermin doing in our seats?" one of the shapes demanded. Its voice wasn't much more than a feral growl, the words barely recognizable. A wolf's head, complete with glistening fangs and yellow eyes, moved near, and Jackie found herself staring at a high-tech version of the Big Bad Wolf. Dressed in battle fatigues and body armor, the creature bristled with weapons, both guns and knives alike. Its partner, a slightly smaller female, looked just as deadly.

"My apologies," Sividious said. "I thought we were on Level 4."

"Well, you're not," the wolf-being growled, obviously spoiling for a fight. "And now we're going to have to wait for a hazmat team to decontaminate our seats."

Jackie was so stunned by the remark—not to mention scared—that she didn't know how to respond. Sividious, on the other hand, laughed. Rising to his feet, he brought the cattle prod to bear, its tip pointed right at the wolf-thing's throat.

"The only thing the hazmat team will need to decontaminate is the section of spectators standing behind you," he growled. "So step aside before I weary of your attitude and paint the concourse with your insides."

Sividious was bluffing, of course, but the wolf-creatures didn't know that, so Jackie hurriedly raised her cattle prod as well. "He said *step aside*," she said, rising to her feet. Only then did the wolf-creatures seem to take note of what she and Sividious were wearing. Two sets of yellow eyes fastened on the black belt around her waist, and both wolf-things dipped their heads in apology.

"Forgive us, Chal'masa," the she-wolf mumbled, and her companion was only a heartbeat behind with an apology of his own.

"We didn't know who you were," he said then slowly backed away down the stairs, his eyes averted, his head lowered.

"You're forgiven," Sividious told them, lowering his cattle prod. He and Jackie started up the stairs, leaving the wolf-beings to stare at them. Their yellow eyes were a mix of awe and relief.

"What does *Chal'masa* mean?" she asked once they were out of earshot.

"Who cares," Sividious whispered. "So long as it makes them fear us."

"But it had something to do with the karate uniforms, right?" she asked, hoping she hadn't imagined it.

"Undoubtedly," he said. "But we'll have to figure that out some other time. Right now I just want to find a quiet place where I can wait for my knees to stop shaking. I've never been so scared in all my life. I thought we were dead."

"You didn't show it," she told him. "That was a great bluff."

He laughed weakly. "It was, wasn't it," he said then laughed again. "Any bluff is great as long as it isn't called. Next time we might not be so lucky."

"Then let's find Aya and leave this messed-up place once and for all."

"I'm right with you, Chal'masa," he said. "I'm right with you."

13
AYA AND THE DRAGON CENTIPEDE

OUT IN THE MAIN CORRIDOR, the crowd had thinned considerably now that most of the spectators had taken their seats. Those who remained were hurriedly purchasing food from the vendors and scurrying toward their respective concourses. Jackie watched a group of legless, slug-like creatures in small hover cars float by, then she turned to Sividious.

"So what's the plan?"

"I don't know," he said. "I was kind of hoping you might have an idea."

She thought back to what the yellow-and-green alien had told them about the Locker Rooms. "Mr. Lemon-Lime back there mentioned the Locker Rooms; maybe we should start there."

Sividious narrowed his eyes thoughtfully. "Unfortunately, I didn't get the impression that the Locker Rooms are rooms with lockers like in a gym. I figure they are more like rooms where people are locked up."

"You mean like a prison?" she asked, a cold, sick feeling washing through her.

"More like a kennel," he frowned. "I get the feeling the Kaladan don't consider the participants of the Games to be much more than animals. Expendable animals. But yes, it would certainly be like a prison."

"So there might be guards."

Sividious shrugged. "Maybe. As automated as the rest of this place is, they might not be needed. Maybe all we need is this." He fingered the AAP. "Remember the white pig thing that rode with us on the elevator? The Jemkalat? He was headed to the lower levels. He had an AAP or something close to it. I'll bet only the Kaladan Agents have truly unlimited access to this place."

"That's not all we need," she told him, frowning. "Access is one thing, but without a clear direction, we could wander in the lower levels forever and never find Aya. We need a map or a blueprint of this place."

Sividious opened his mouth to respond, but the voice of the beautiful woman announcer sounded from outside, cutting him off.

"Citizens of the universe," she said. "I have just been informed of a change in today's events. Due to a recent interstellar conflict in the Telmara Galaxy, several participants in the Sproark Invitational are unable to attend. Therefore, we will move directly to the Jomon Worlds of Magic semifinal and the contest between Aya the Kelsprite and Shoar the Dragon Centipede."

Jackie locked eyes with Sividious and saw the same sick feeling that was washing through her. He looked like he wanted to swear.

"Crap!" he breathed. "What are we going to do now?"

Jackie shook her head. "The only thing we can do, I guess," she told him. "Watch, and hope she survives." Her stomach was tight as she spoke, and she felt like she was going to throw up. *The Dragon Centipede wouldn't really kill her, would it? The Kaladan and their spectators couldn't be so depraved as to actually allow participants to die, could they?* She could see by the anguished frown on Sividious's face that he was thinking the same thing.

"It will be okay," she said, trying to reassure him. "She'll win, and then we will find out where she is and free her."

"She won't win," Sividious said softly, then continued before Jackie could protest. "Not without help."

Jackie blinked her surprise. "Help? What can we do?"

"We can give her hope," Sividious answered. "When Aya gave me the AAP, she was tired and desperate and had pretty much given up already. If we can get close enough to the playing field for her to see me, she'll know that I took her seriously enough to try to help. Maybe the prospect of being rescued will give her the strength she needs to win the match."

"And if not?" Jackie asked before she thought better of it. She saw Sividious stiffen and hurriedly took him by the arm. "I'm sorry," she said. "I didn't really mean that. Of course she'll survive. Tell me your plan."

"We go to Level 1," he said. "The AAP will get us that far. We'll have to hope that our appearance as Chal'masa—whatever the heck that is—will keep people from asking too many questions."

They hurried toward the elevator but spotted a stairwell instead. They pushed through the doors and raced down the stairs two at a time. Once on Level 1, they crossed the corridor to the concourse and paused to look for a couple of empty seats. They found one section on the very front row that was unoccupied and started down toward it. Only when they reached it did they see that it was cordoned off with a pulsating field of yellow energy. Green holographic lettering scrolled across the surface, announcing that the row was reserved for the prime minister of Zolaazezzer and his guests.

Jackie was about to turn back when Sividious reached into his uniform and removed the AAP. Without the slightest concern for who might be watching, he touched it against the holographic lettering and deactivated the energy field.

"Lady Molenshire," he said, tucking the AAP away and motioning her forward. "Your seat awaits."

Ignoring the startled looks of those seated behind them, Jackie moved to the second seat and gazed aloofly out over the playing field. Sividious took the seat next to her and did the same. From the corner of her eye, Jackie saw the satisfied smile on his face.

"If you act like you know what you are doing," he whispered, "people usually assume that you do."

"What if the prime minister and his guests show up?" she asked quietly.

"We'll play stupid," he replied. "But chances are, if they aren't here by now, they aren't coming."

"Good point," she said, then turned her attention to the playing field. The smooth green surface—she thought it looked like grass—was sprouting a variety of shapes. There were pillars and walls and blocks, all of which appeared from somewhere below ground to form an array of obstacles. A second set of obstacles floated in from a side passage to hover at various heights above the playing field. Some, Jackie noted, were covered with spikes or rows of razor-sharp blades.

"That doesn't look good," Sividious mumbled, and Jackie put her hand on his arm to comfort him.

"At least it will be as dangerous for the Dragon Centipede as it will be for Aya," she said.

"Will it?" Sividious asked, indicating the large shape emerging from one of the ground-level passages.

Long as a school bus and armored like a battleship, Shoar the Dragon Centipede moved toward the center of the arena in an undulating blur of legs and glossy black segments. His large mandibles glistened with what looked like poison. Three sets of leathery wings ran the length of his body, quivering with anticipation. The dozen or so armored segments of his body sported nearly as many spikes and razor-sharp edges as the obstacles floating above the arena.

The crowd booed mightily as Shoar neared the center of the playing field, and the Dragon Centipede reacted by whipping its tail end around and smashing one of the smaller walls into splintered fragments.

"This is definitely not looking good," Sividious muttered again.

A moment later Aya appeared from a passage below and to the right of where Jackie and Sividious sat. The crowd erupted, cheering and shouting her name. Flowers were tossed toward her by adoring fans, but the young Kelsprite barely noticed. Her eyes were fixed on Shoar, and her face was resigned. She had the look of someone walking to the gallows.

Sividious had been right, Jackie realized. Aya had already given up.

A bright light began flashing from atop the box seats, and the crowd slowly quieted in response to it. Seeing his chance, Sividious leaned over the railing and called Aya's name.

She didn't look up, of course, so used to hearing her name that she simply dismissed the lone voice as an overzealous fan.

"Aya," Sividious called again. "It's me. I've come to keep my promise."

This time Aya looked, and her eyes went wide with recognition. They narrowed just as quickly, and her slender blue jaw tightened with determination. She nodded to let Sividious know she'd heard him, then turned and started toward the center of the arena. There was a quickness to her gait, a confidence that only moments before had been absent. Sividious had given her hope. He had given her a reason to keep fighting.

But as Jackie watched the young Kelsprite near the center of the arena, as she saw how tiny and helpless-looking Aya was in the presence of her opponent, a cold knot of fear tightened in her chest. Hope had given Aya the will to continue to fight, but hope alone would never be enough to defeat a creature like Shoar. It was an awful thought, but Jackie couldn't imagine how Aya would survive.

She glanced at Sividious to see his face pinched with worry. His white-knuckled grip on the cattle prod showed he was contemplating leaping into the arena to help Aya.

"She'll be all right," Jackie whispered. "She's got the crowd on her side."

Sividious frowned. "But the Kaladan are rooting for Shoar."

Aya reached the center of the arena and stepped up onto a blue platform that had risen from the playing field. Opposite her, the Dragon Centipede took its place atop a red platform.

"Citizens of the universe," the female announcer said from the video screen, "I give you Aya the Kelsprite and Shoar the Dragon Centipede."

The words had scarcely left her mouth when Shoar lunged forward in a blur of legs and glossy black segments, so deceptively quick for his size that he reached the blue platform before anyone in the stadium even had time to cry out.

Aya, however, was even faster, and Shoar's mandibles closed on the empty spot the tiny Kelsprite had occupied only a nanosecond before. Her leap carried her high into the air, and she disappeared behind a floating obstacle in a flash of blue wings.

The crowd celebrated the narrow escape, but there was an edge of nervousness to the sound, the unmistakable sound of fear. Aya may be the crowd favorite, but those gathered to watch her had no illusions that she was the underdog here today.

Shoar's long body rolled back on itself as he tried to follow Aya's movements, and green venom sprayed the air like rain. Wings extending, he lifted skyward in pursuit, his legs tucked beneath his segmented body.

Keeping the floating obstacles between herself and her opponent, Aya flew higher, her delicate wings beating the air like those of a hummingbird. No sooner had Shoar's head cleared the first obstacle than she struck, hammering the Dragon Centipede with a torrent of blue-white flame. It shot from her outstretched hands as from a flamethrower, vaporizing Shoar's spray of venom and turning him aside as if he'd been struck with a hammer.

Jackie shielded her eyes against the brightness, so stunned by what she'd just witnessed that she was unable to speak.

Sividious, on the other hand, jumped as if he'd been kicked. "Holy crap!" he exclaimed, "Did you feel that?" His eyes were wide, but Jackie was unable to determine if it was from excitement or fear. His gaze was still fastened on Aya.

"Did I feel what?" she asked. When he didn't answer, she slugged him in the shoulder to get his attention. "Did I feel what?"

"What Aya just did," he said. "It felt like . . . it felt like . . ." He stopped, frowning. "I don't know *what* it felt like," he admitted. "I only know I felt it. Not on the outside, like when you feel the thud of fireworks, but on the inside—a fiery tingle that washed through me as she readied her attack."

Before Jackie could respond, Sividious whipped his head back in the direction of the battle. "There it is again," he said. "Aya's getting ready to do something."

And she did, attacking Shoar's first set of wings with a stream of fire that burned them to ash and peeled a segment of the monster's armor away to reveal a steaming patch of gray-green flesh.

The crowd shrieked wildly at this, and Jackie looked around to find faces filled with a frenzied light. These people—these creatures, she corrected—actually enjoyed this. They enjoyed the brutality of the conflict, its pain and anger and violence. They enjoyed cheering for Aya and wanted her to win. But, Jackie realized with horror, cheering for Aya's victory meant they were cheering for Shoar's defeat. She could see in their faces that they wanted the Dragon Centipede to die.

"This is wrong," she whispered to Sividious. "We have to stop this."

But Sividious didn't hear her, his attention so firmly fastened on what was happening that she could have hit him with the cattle prod and he wouldn't have noticed. His eyes were filled with a wild light as well, not of enjoyment or excitement, thankfully, but a wild light nonetheless. His hands were pressed tightly against his chest, and he was breathing in ragged, uneven gulps.

"Shoar's doing something now," he muttered. "I can feel it."

Feel it? she thought, then flinched as a ripple of red energy surged outward from Shoar's head in a thin, disk-like wave. It ripped through four of the floating obstacles as if they were made of glass, sending shards of rock and metal hurtling toward the upper levels of spectators.

Jackie opened her mouth to scream, but a massive energy shield activated to repel the shrapnel. Those seated behind the shield barely even flinched as the deadly missiles thumped against it, the smaller ones vanishing in flashes of fire, the larger ones trailing smoke as they tumbled toward the playing field.

Aya managed to avoid the strike of energy from Shoar, but she was caught in a spray of stone from one of the splintered obstacles. The debris hammered into her like the blast from a giant shotgun, crumpling her like a wounded bird and hurtling her backward through the air. The crowd gave a collective gasp of horror as she glanced off the side of a floating obstacle and plummeted toward the floor of the arena, her wings flapping with wounded desperation. She hit the green surface of the playing field and lay still.

A hushed silence fell over the spectators, and Jackie took a quick look around to see the dread that painted nearly every face.

Shoar settled to the ground a few yards away and folded his two remaining sets of wings. The hush blanketing the crowd turned to murmurs of disbelief as the Dragon Centipede turned its beady red gaze on the fallen Kelsprite and moved in for the kill.

"She's faking it," Sividious said, sounding so certain that Jackie turned to look at him.

"What?"

"She wove a shield of magic to protect herself from the stone shards. Her fall was deliberate and controlled."

"How do you know?" she asked.

"I felt it," he answered, his eyes still fastened on Aya.

"It's got to be the AAP," she told him. "Somehow it lets you feel the magic."

He nodded absently. "That must be it," he said, but he didn't sound too sure. Before Jackie could press the issue further, Shoar reached Aya.

14
MAGIC AND MERCY

"That must be it," Sividious heard himself say, but he knew it wasn't true. The AAP was tucked inside his uniform, not hanging around his neck. This was something else entirely, something that allowed him to feel what Aya was going to do, to sense the magic she wielded. He didn't know what that something might be, and right now he didn't have time to wonder about it. Shoar had reached Aya.

The Dragon Centipede's mandibles clacked loudly in anticipation as the front third of his body reared up, his rows of legs waving, his beady red eyes glowing with victory. Tilting his wedge-like head toward Aya, Shoar prepared to strike.

Sividious felt Aya's magic before he saw it, a tingling flow of warm energy that surged through his chest and made him inhale sharply. A heartbeat later, Aya's arms came up and Shoar was knocked backward by a wall of white-hot fire. It incinerated his remaining two sets of wings in a flash of smoke and hurled him into a stone pillar. The pillar burst apart in a spray of dust, the larger fragments tearing gashes in the lush grass and punching holes in a nearby wall.

Shoar coiled in on himself, trying to protect the areas where his armor had been damaged. Sividious could see where several more sections of the creature's exoskeleton had been stripped away, revealing the soft flesh beneath.

Writhing beneath the torrent of Aya's magic, Shoar tried to launch a counterattack, but the red flames sputtered and died beneath the onslaught of the tiny Kelsprite's relentless fire.

The Dragon Centipede was weakening, Sividious realized. In a moment, his strength would fail completely . . . and he would be dead.

The thought sent a sudden wave of sympathy washing through him, and he shook his head sadly. *Jackie was right,* he thought. This entire competition was wrong. Fighting to the death was wrong. The Games of the Kaladan were corrupt and evil and needed to be stopped.

He frowned. But who was he to do such a thing? In light of the power wielded by the Kaladan, who were any of the thousands upon thousands who were witnessing these horrible Games? No one could stop this. Most of those present probably didn't even want to. They wanted Aya to kill the monstrous centipede. They were cheering for it.

But Aya, bless her little blue heart, was not like the multitude calling for Shoar's death, and the torrent of magic she wielded faded to a trickle. Tendrils of flame still danced above Shoar's quivering body, but they no longer touched him. Cautiously, the creature's massive head slipped from between his coiled segments to regard Aya without blinking. A surprised hush fell over the crowd as they waited to see what Aya would do next.

The young Kelsprite turned toward the box seats. Her voice, amplified by the stadium's technology, reached the ears of all who watched.

"This match is over," she said softly. "I will not kill this creature. I will not satisfy the bloodlust of the Kaladan."

She started to say something else, but the voice amplifier cut off, leaving the crowd to sit in stunned silence.

"That's gonna tick some people off," Jackie muttered.

Yeah, Sividious thought, *the Kaladan.*

And then someone a few rows away shouted. "Praised be the Kelsprite for her mercy! Praised be the name of Aya!"

"Praise be to Aya!" another voice shouted, and from somewhere above came another cry. "Aya the Merciful."

Within seconds the entire stadium was on its feet chanting. "Aya! Aya! Aya!"

Down on the playing field, the obstacles began slipping back out of sight, and those floating in the air moved toward the openings from which they had emerged. A set of doors opened at ground level, and a dozen figures wearing armor and bearing the crackling batons carried by the Kaladan Agents moved forward to surround Shoar. Sividious couldn't be sure because of the hoods hiding their faces, but he suspected they were the same fish-faced creatures who'd come to Earth hunting Aya.

The giant centipede, his gaze still fastened on the tiny Kelsprite, uncoiled his body and let himself be led away by his baton-wielding escort. He disappeared into a tunnel and was lost from view.

"What will happen to him now?" Jackie wondered aloud, but Sividious didn't have an answer. Nor did he have an answer for what he had felt regarding Aya's use of magic. And that, he realized, scared him more than anything.

It scared him because there was no logical explanation for any of it. And he needed it to be logical—he needed it to be scientific. Facts and details—the laws of physics and nature and mathematics. He needed an explanation he could get his mind around. Magic wasn't real. It couldn't be.

He looked around the stadium. He had accepted this place as real because it obviously obeyed the laws written about by Einstein in his theories of time and space. But magic? No way. There had to be some other explanation for what Aya was able to do.

A squat, turtle-like creature with a giraffe neck leaned forward to answer Jackie's question, interrupting Sividious's thoughts.

"The Kaladan don't much care for losers," the creature said, looking around conspiratorially. "But they will send him to the medical facilities, where he will be healed. That way he will be strong and healthy when they send him to the Kaladan homeworld to work in the mines." The squat body hunched in such a way as to indicate a shrug. "Aya didn't do Shoar any favors by sparing his life. A week or two in the mines will make him wish Aya had killed him."

With that, the creature activated what appeared to be some kind of hovercraft and floated away up the stairs.

Sividious and Jackie watched him go then turned their attention back to Aya. She had moved back to the blue platform, where she was being approached by a pair of slender females wearing elegant red dresses and bearing flowers. They looked to be from the same world as the female announcer, with their purple skin and jet-black hair. They reached Aya and presented her with the flowers.

"Citizens of the universe," the announcer said, her face appearing on the video screen. "I give you our semifinal champion, Aya the Kelsprite from the world of Fallisor of the Promor Galaxy."

The crowd cheered loud and long, stopping only after the lights atop the box seats started to flash, the signal for them to quiet.

"Join us next week for the final round of the Jomon Worlds of Magic Tournament, where Aya will face either Lazacor the Rock Troll of Doromara or Sheylie the Kelsprite from Aya's homeworld of Fallisor."

There was a collective gasp of surprise from the crowd, and Sividious looked around to see eyes of every shape, color, and size going wide with shock.

"You heard right, folks," the announcer said dramatically. "We have the possibility of a match between two beings from the same world. This is a result of Grom the Fire Wraith being disqualified for artificially enhancing his magic abilities with technology. His replacement was drawn at random from a pool of participants. Check your holoprogram for more details." She smiled sweetly. "It just goes to show that there is never a dull moment at the Kaladan Stadium between Worlds."

The video screen went dark, and the strange hum that sounded like a radio being tuned to a different channel echoed through the stadium. And just like that, the words of all those around Sividious became indistinguishable once more.

"Drawn at random, my eye," Sividious said disgustedly, pulling the AAP from within his karate robe and placing it around his neck. After checking to make sure he could understand those around him, he tucked the AAP inside the uniform where it would be out of sight. He turned to Jackie. "The Kaladan are rigging everything to try to bring Aya down. There is no way she will fight one of her own kind, and they know it. She showed her one true 'weakness' when she refused to kill the Dragon Centipede. The Kaladan are going to use her compassion against her. She will either be killed or be sent to the mines."

Jackie nodded, her face twisted with anger. "What do you want to bet that this Sheylie has no such reservations about killing and would be more than happy to remove Aya from the Games?"

"I don't think we'll have to worry about that," Sividious said as he examined the flickering images of the holoprogram he'd pulled from its slot on the underside of his chair. "It says right here that Sheylie is Aya's cousin."

"Her cousin?" Jackie muttered. "Sividious, what are we going to do?"

"We're going to keep our promise," he said firmly. "We're getting Aya out of here."

"And Sheylie?" Jackie asked.

Sividious felt his resolve tighten. "We'll get her out too."

15
THE LOWER LEVELS

As the lights began to dim and the crowd made its way toward the exits, Aya watched the boy from Portal T16. He stood with a female his same age, and the two were studying the breaking news flashing across the shimmering surface of a holoprogram.

Breaking news, indeed, she thought angrily. The Kaladan Agents had captured her cousin more than a week ago. A week of time as measured here in the stadium, she amended; on her homeworld only a single day would have passed since Sheylie's disappearance. Her parents might not yet even realize she was missing.

She glanced at the boy and wondered how much time had passed on his world before he had decided to come and help her. Not much, she decided. He had the look of someone who acted quickly on what he knew he needed to do. She was lucky to have found him.

The blue platform she was standing on began to sink back into the playing field—a sign from her captors that it was time to return to her cell—and she started across the playing field toward the dark opening that led to the lower levels. She didn't angle straight for it but took advantage of a debris pile left by the battle to move toward the boy from Portal T16.

He saw her coming and leaned forward over the rail as she neared. He spoke to her, but his words were gibberish in her ears. She tapped her ear and shook her head meaningfully.

"I can't understand you right now," she told him. "But I know you can understand me, so listen." She glanced around to make sure there weren't any Agents nearby. "I am being held on Sublevel 12 in Section F. All the doors and security points are automated so you should have no trouble gaining access with the AAP. But be careful. There is a lot of activity down there. And there are armed guards and sometimes Agents."

The boy nodded his understanding, then his eyes moved pointedly in the direction from which she'd come. She glanced over her shoulder and found three Kaladan Agents approaching.

She looked back at the boy. "Thank you for coming," she told him then moved toward the tunnel.

* * *

As Aya started for the tunnel, Sividious turned his attention to the three Agents striding across the playing field. They didn't seem overly concerned that the Kelsprite had spoken to him and may not have realized that she had. There were so many adoring fans vying for her attention that he was just one of a thousand faces in the crowd. Still, it would be better not to take any chances.

"Come on," he said to Jackie. "I'll tell you what she said after we are out of sight of the Agents."

They strode up the stairs into the main corridor then moved to a quiet nook near the stairwell. "Aya is down on Sublevel 12," he told her, "in Section F of the Locker Rooms." He glanced around guardedly. "She said that the AAP will allow us access but that we need to be careful. Apparently, the lower levels don't shut down after a competition the same way the upper levels do. There will be a lot more people, uh . . . I mean beings, than there are up here. She said there may be Agents as well."

He looked Jackie in the eyes. "You don't have to come if you don't want to."

"Oh, I'm coming all right," she insisted. "I didn't come this far to turn back now."

Sividious looked at his watch. "We've been here for just over an hour," he told her. "That means only about twenty minutes have passed back on Earth. If we do this quickly, we can get Aya and her cousin out of here and be back home before an hour of Earth time has passed."

"And then what?" Jackie asked.

Sividious stared at her. He knew what she was thinking, and he couldn't deny that he had already considered it himself. Tempting as the thought was, however, he simply didn't believe that two kids from Earth could free everyone the Kaladan had imprisoned here. He shrugged. "We'll cross that bridge when we get to it. First, we have to save Aya."

Bidding Jackie to follow, he moved to the elevator and pressed the down button. The doors opened, and he and Jackie moved inside. A willowy creature with bark-like skin and grass-colored hair nodded to them as they entered, but it didn't speak. An Access Pass similar to the one worn by the Jemkalat hung around its stick-like neck.

Nodding a greeting in return, Sividious pushed the button for Sublevel 12 then studied the creature from the corner of his eye, trying to decide if it was male or female.

At Sublevel 5, the doors opened and the tree creature exited, leaving Sividious and Jackie alone.

"You know," Jackie said after the doors had closed, "some of these things freak me out worse than others. And walking trees just went to the top of my list." She shook her head. "The sooner we get out of here, the better."

Sividious nodded. "I won't argue with that."

They fell quiet as the elevator neared Sublevel 12, and Sividious tightened his grip on the cattle prod. He saw Jackie do the same. A moment later the doors opened, and they moved through into a well-lighted room.

A handful of beings occupied the room, some lounging on a collection of sofas to the left of the elevator, some clustered around a bank of computers. Those lounging on the sofas turned to stare at him and Jackie then quickly busied themselves with something else when they noticed how they were dressed.

The Chal'masa thing again, he realized, once again grateful for the karate uniforms.

Those at the computers, however, didn't even look up, so engrossed in what they were doing that they failed to notice the new arrivals. Sividious listened for a moment, and a wave of anger washed through him when he realized they were discussing the buying and selling of competitors for one of the upcoming competitions.

Filthy slavers, he thought, outraged by the very notion of owning another being. It made him want to jab each of them with the cattle prod.

Gaining control of his anger, he dismissed the slavers from his thoughts and glanced about the rest of the chamber. Shaped like a half-moon, it had openings for a dozen or so corridors. The corridors—some lighted, others cloaked in shadow—stretched away into the distance like the spokes of a wheel. Every one of the openings was warded against entry by a flickering energy shield.

Moving shapes were visible in some of the corridors, but Sividious had no way of knowing if these were more of those who owned the competitors or if they were the competitors themselves. He offered a silent prayer that none of them were Kaladan Agents.

"So which way do we go?" Jackie whispered, and Sividious pointed to the corridor directly across from where they had come in.

As they started across the room, Sividious studied the array of passes he saw hanging about the different beings' necks, but he didn't see any that even remotely resembled an AAP. Like the Jemkalat they'd met earlier, these beings likely had limited access to this part of the stadium. And yet they were still creatures to be reckoned with, as evidenced by their status as owners instead of competitors. He and Jackie would need to watch how they acted around them.

The energy shield deactivated at their approach—a result of the All Access Pass, Sividious knew—and he and Jackie moved into the corridor without hesitating. No sooner had they cleared the door's framework than the energy shield sprang back into place. When they were well away from the antechamber, Sividious turned to Jackie.

"Those gathered at the computers were buying and selling people like Aya and her cousin," he told her, his voice laced with disgust. "I heard them talking about it."

Jackie looked at the AAP hanging around his neck. "The sooner I get one of those, the better," she told him. "I hate not being able to understand what's being said around me."

"That reminds me," he said. "We need to be careful what we say within earshot of others. Some of them might have passes with language translation abilities, and we certainly don't need them learning of our plans to free Aya. They would turn us over to the Kaladan in a heartbeat." He scowled back over his shoulder. "People like those we saw at the computers would sell their own mothers."

They continued down the corridor without speaking, passing doors marked *Maintenance* and *Supplies*, but there was nothing to indicate this was a cellblock of any kind. They passed a large set of steel doors marked with the word *Danger*, and Sividious stopped to press his ear against them to listen. The hum of machines was audible within, a steady sound that made him think of generators. A power source, most likely, he decided. Probably for the energy shields on the cellblocks. It would be nice to know for sure, but he didn't have time to go inside for a look.

He and Jackie started walking again, and the end of the corridor eventually took shape as another of the shimmering blue energy shields.

It deactivated at their approach, and he and Jackie moved through to the room beyond.

It was a large room, a good forty paces wide and shaped like an octagon. Each of the eight walls had a large doorway shielded by an energy field, and the corridors beyond stretched away into darkness. In the center of the room stood a raised command center, a pedestal of computer and video screens, and banks of red and green lights. And there, seated in the midst of it all, was a Jemkalat. And not just any Jemkalat, Sividious realized with a start, but the one they'd shared a ride with on the elevator.

"This might complicate things," he whispered to Jackie then waited to see what would happen.

16
AN UNEXPECTED TOUR

THE JEMKALAT'S BOAR-LIKE FACE BROKE into a smile when he saw them, and he rose and moved down a narrow set of steps on one side of the command center.

"So, you've come to see where I work, have you?" he said, and Sividious translated the creature's words for Jackie.

When the Jemkalat saw this, he returned to the command center and pulled open a small storage compartment. He withdrew a lanyard with an Access Pass similar to the one he wore, handed it to Jackie, then waited while she put it on.

"That should help with communication," the Jemkalat said, and Jackie nodded.

"It does," she told him. "Thank you."

"I'll need it back when we are done with the tour," the boar-faced creature said. "It is a guest pass only."

"Tour?" Jackie asked.

"Isn't that why you are here?"

"Yes, it is," Sividious answered, seeing his chance to learn more about the stadium.

"Well, then," the Jemkalat said, sounding pleased. "Where should we start? With names, I suppose. I'm Loshar Uublakoria. I'm a Jemkalat from the world of Essel in the Markarian Galaxy. I'm sure you know the name; it's the same galaxy that houses the homeworld of the Kaladan." He paused, looking them over and waiting expectantly.

"I'm Albert Einstein from the world of Tatooine in the Yoda Galaxy," Sividious told him. "My friend here is Marie Curie, also from Tatooine."

"Never heard of either place," Loshar replied, "but that doesn't mean much. It is a big universe, after all. And getting bigger—just like the stadium. Why, the Kaladan have added a dozen new portals just since the start of the Jomon Worlds of Magic Tournament."

He looked at their karate uniforms. "Tatooine, you say? With those clothes, I would have guessed you were from Roshamir in the Aillorius Galaxy."

"We are often mistaken for Chal'masa," Sividious told him, "but we aren't going to alter our way of dress because of it."

"Nor should you," Loshar told him. "And there are, shall we say, certain benefits to looking like the deadliest group of assassins to ever walk the corridors of this magnificent stadium."

"Would the Chal'masa be offended by our manner of dress?" Jackie asked.

"Hard to say," Loshar said. "But I don't think so. They would probably assume you earned the belt and are a force to be reckoned with just as they are."

"People do keep their distance," Sividious said then smiled. "So how about that tour?"

Loshar's tiny eyes narrowed as he smiled. "What would you like to see?"

"Whatever you have time to show us," Sividious replied. "But I know Marie here would like to see where they keep Aya the Kelsprite. She is a really big fan."

"Then you are in luck," Loshar told her, "because she is housed in this very section."

He started toward a passage at the far side of the octagonal chamber. "This way," he said. "Follow me."

"This is too easy," Jackie whispered just loudly enough for Sividious to hear.

He nodded, but he wasn't going to get too excited about things until he could decide what they should do next. From the way Jackie was holding the cattle prod, it looked as though she was contemplating using it on Loshar, but Sividious didn't think now was the time. Besides, the Jemkalat was the nearest thing they had to a friend in this place; it might be best if they didn't ruin that.

He touched her cattle prod with his own and shook his head in warning.

When she frowned at him, Sividious realized he'd been right about what she was thinking. She did relax her hold on the weapon, though, and for that he was grateful.

With Loshar in the lead, they passed dozens of holding cells, all of them occupied, all of them shielded by sheets of shimmering blue energy. The occupants—the prisoners, Sividious corrected—watched them pass without speaking, their faces worried.

"These are the Locker Rooms for the Draftees," Loshar told them. "The Free Agents are housed in Sections L through Z. It is the same on each of the Sublevels: A through K for the Draftees, L through Z for Free Agents."

"What is the difference between the two?" Jackie asked then flinched as Loshar turned to study her curiously. He didn't speak, but his eyes seemed to say, *You don't seem to know very much about how things work, do you?*

Sividious realized they needed to be careful not to show too great a lack of understanding about the stadium lest Loshar become suspicious about why they had access to the sublevels.

"Free Agents are competitors who choose to compete in the Games," Loshar said. "Some choose to compete because of a sense of duty; they are patriots who want to represent their homeworld, to showcase their world's honor and tradition. Some do it to champion a cause or settle military or political disputes. Why, in the last year alone, several wars were settled by a duel between two combatants instead of through full-scale military conflict." He shrugged. "Most of the Free Agents, however, do it for the money and the fame."

He gestured to the bank of holding cells stretching away into the distance. "The Draftees, on the other hand, are here against their will. Some are recruited by the Kaladan Agents because they have skills the Kaladan believe will make for good entertainment. Some are sent here by the authorities of their homeworlds—a type of exile, I suppose, for committing criminal acts. Some are purchased through trade agreements between neighboring worlds or systems."

Purchased, Sividious thought, his anger deepening, *like pets from a pet store or livestock from a fair.* The idea of sentient life-forms being purchased so they could be used as entertainment made him want to puke. Beside him, Jackie's expression was equally sour.

"And the Draftees that lose," Sividious said, "they're sent to the Kaladan homeworld to work in the mines, are they not?"

Loshar nodded without turning around. "Some of them are," he agreed. "Some are cycled back through the Games in later competitions, especially if they have gained a following among the spectators."

"Like Aya the Kelsprite?" Jackie asked.

"Aya is a completely different story," the Jemkalat said, sounding displeased. "Yes, she has a following, a very large following, in fact. But she did something to anger the Kaladan. No matter how well she does in the Games, even if she wins the Jomon tournament, she will likely still end up in the mines."

"What did she do?" Jackie asked.

Loshar shrugged his massive shoulders. "I have no idea."

"I overheard some of the spectators talking about Aya," Sividious said. "They believe the Kaladan are trying to rig the competition so that Aya suffers an awful death in the jaws of something like the Dragon Centipede."

"Dangerous words, those," Loshar told him, turning around so he could look into his face. "The Kaladan pride themselves on fairness. They would not take kindly to any accusation that they were trying to unfairly eliminate a competitor."

"I'm just telling you what I heard," Sividious said.

"Even so," Loshar cautioned, "some things are better left unsaid."

He faced forward once more, and Sividious and Jackie followed in silence, exchanging looks that showed what they thought of so-called Kaladan fairness.

A moment later Loshar stopped in front of a holding cell. The energy shield had been deactivated, and the interior of the cell was dark and empty.

"It looks like Aya has not yet returned from her competition with Shoar," the Jemkalat told them. "They must have taken her to the medical facilities for healing." He gave Jackie a look of sympathy. "I'm sorry you weren't able to see her."

"That's okay," Jackie said, sounding truly disappointed. "Some other time, perhaps."

"You two are welcome to come back anytime," Loshar said. "My shift doesn't end for ten more hours, but I doubt Aya will be back before I leave. Once a competitor is taken to the medical facilities, they are usually kept overnight, so she probably won't be back until tomorrow. My next shift is the day after tomorrow. Unlike today, where I'm working the swing shift, I'll have the graveyard shift that day. You could come back then if you'd like."

"We might," Sividious told him. He paused as if considering something. "That reminds me," he said, knowing that what he was about to ask was risky but deciding to take a chance anyway. "I've misplaced my time chart. You wouldn't happen to have an extra one would you?"

When Loshar frowned, Sividious cringed inwardly, his stomach tightening. "Time chart?" the Jemakalat asked. "I'm not sure I know what you mean."

"It was a chart that showed the time differentials between the various worlds and the stadium, as well as between the various worlds themselves."

"Oh," Loshar said. "Now I know what you mean." He laughed. "It's called an astronomical almanac," he told them then laughed once more. "You have a unique way of speaking, Albert," he said. "It is simple and refreshing." He nodded his head. "Yes, I'm sure I have an extra one lying around somewhere back at the command center. I'll get it for you at the end of the tour."

He gestured down the corridor with one of his radish-like arms. "Shall we continue?"

"Please," Sividious replied, motioning Loshar to resume the lead.

The Jemkalat smiled his enthusiasm and started away. Sividious and Jackie moved to follow, but as they did, Sividious glanced at the lettering on the wall above the door to Aya's cell.

F7-55R

I'll be back, he told the empty cell, a plan already starting to form in his mind. They would free Aya tomorrow when Loshar was no longer on duty. The Kaladan would be furious about Aya's escape, and Sividious didn't want Loshar to have to pay the price of their wrath.

Yes, he pitied the poor soul who would be on duty tomorrow, but it couldn't be helped. Besides, he added, trying to console himself, anyone who willingly worked for the Kaladan had already assumed the risks of what displeasing them might mean. Even Loshar.

And yet, Sividious would do what he could to keep the Jemkalat free of blame. In light of everything the boar-faced creature was doing for them, they owed him that much at least.

17
GATES AND ALMANACS

JACKIE'S THOUGHTS WERE DARK AS she followed the Jemkalat through the remainder of their tour of the holding cells. She was disappointed that Aya hadn't been in her cell. She would have loved to see her, to tell her with a smile and a wink that they would be coming for her.

She glanced at Sividious and found his face unreadable. She wished she knew what he was thinking. She wished she knew if he had a plan. But she didn't dare speak to him about any of it until they were away from Loshar. Anyone who worked for the Kaladan as a guard in their stinking prison was not to be trusted.

The energy field at the end of the cellblock Loshar was leading them through deactivated at their approach, and they moved on into a chamber a hundred yards wide and forty or fifty feet high. Filled with beings and machines of every shape and size, it was a dizzying scene of both ground and airborne traffic—a massive, warehouse-like corridor that curved away to the left and right as far as the eye could see.

The far wall, which Jackie supposed to be the outer edge of Sublevel 12, shimmered with portals large enough for a semitruck to pass through. The area in front of each portal was cordoned off with an energy shield and rows of flashing lights set in the floor. Even as she watched, one of the portals flashed brightly, and a large antigravity sled appeared within the protected area in front of it, loaded with crates of various sizes, many of which were marked with the words *Live Specimens*.

The red-skinned humanoid who had appeared with the sled, and who appeared to be guiding it by remote control, used his Access Pass to deactivate the energy shield, then guided the sled away from the landing area and down the corridor.

"Those are the gates," Loshar told them. "They are used when anything larger than a standard life-form needs entrance into the stadium.

Take Shoar the Dragon Centipede, for instance. He is too big and too dangerous to be allowed access to the upper levels. Semisentient creatures are much too unpredictable in their behavior. And Shoar is nothing compared to some of the creatures the Talent Scouts have brought in."

He pointed to the departing red-skinned alien and his cargo. "And as you saw with the arrival of the Hremlins on the sled there, the gates are also used for moving goods and merchandise between various worlds. The Kaladan make more money on tariffs than they do on ticket sales."

A Godzilla-like roar echoed toward them, and Jackie turned to see a monstrous, dinosaur-like creature being led through the commotion by a squad of heavily muscled and heavily armored creatures. Troll-like, with stumpy heads and large, luminous eyes, each of the armored creatures held the end of a chain in one hand and a crackling energy wand in the other. The chains were fastened to metal collars around the dinosaur creature's neck.

"What is *that?*" Jackie asked.

Loshar shrugged. "I have no idea, but I'll bet it was expensive."

"Tell me more about the gates," Sividious said, speaking for the first time in quite a while. "Are they as numerous as the portals in the upper levels?"

"There are exactly the same number of gates as there are portals," Loshar answered. "On the stadium side of the wormhole link, that is. On the other side of the portal—the homeworld side—there can be hundreds or even thousands. It depends on how many entry points the Kaladan create for each world."

Jackie did little to hide her surprise. "Let me get this straight," she said. "Here in the stadium there is only one gate and one portal leading to any given world, but there are potentially thousands of gates and portals leading to the stadium from each of those worlds?"

The Jemkalat seemed amused. "Pretty neat, isn't it?"

"But how is that possible?"

Loshar turned to stare at her. "That is something only the Kaladan know."

Jackie frowned at him. "So how does the portal know to deposit me back where I entered as opposed to a portal link in some other city?"

"That's an easy one," the Jemkalat said then flinched as an explosion rocked the chamber. Jackie flinched as well, so startled by the noise that she gave a little yip of fright. She and Sividious and Loshar looked in the direction of the noise to see a ball of smoke mushrooming upward toward the ceiling. Several nearby pallets of merchandise were on fire, and the beings in the area were scrambling for cover as a team of firefighting robots detached themselves from their wall compartments and rushed forward to fight the flames, their hose-like arms spraying green liquid.

"That's why you never let a Gordorian Firetoad get too close to Heishari fireworks," Loshar said, dismissing the commotion as he turned back to Sividious. "As I was saying, that's an easy one. Whenever you enter the stadium, the portal reads your Access Pass or ticket and records the point of entry. When you leave the stadium to return home, the portal retrieves that information and returns you to where you started."

He looked at Jackie. "That's why it would be bad if you tried to return to your homeworld with the Access Pass that I let you borrow. Without a point of entry recorded in its memory chip, it would drop you back into your world at random."

He must have read the startled look on her face because he added, "Fortunately, every kind of Access Pass is programmable. It wouldn't make sense that if every time you wanted to visit a new world you had to enter blind, would it? To pick a destination, all you have to do is visit any one of the stadium's computers, pull up the schematic of the world you want to visit, and enter the coordinates."

He turned to Sividious, his pig eyes critical. When he spoke, his voice held a trace of scorn. "You really should provide your guests with more information before you bring them here," he scolded. "The little dear is obviously troubled about not knowing how things operate."

"I'll do better next time," Sividious promised.

Loshar nodded as if he thought that would be a good idea. "There isn't much more to see," he said. "Every level is pretty much the same. The critical systems are located in the center—power, life-support, and such. Then come the lounges and apartments of the Owners, Talent Scouts, and Agents—you saw those when you exited the elevator onto this level. After the lounges come the Locker Rooms, and after those the corridor of gates." He made a grand gesture at the sight before them. "Where we are now."

"Well, thank you for the tour," Sividious said.

Jackie echoed, "Yes, thank you."

"My pleasure," Loshar said. "Now, if you will accompany me back to my work station, I will collect your guest pass, Miss Curie. And for you, Mr. Einstein, I will round up an astronomical almanac."

As Jackie and Sividious followed in the Jemkalat's wake, the talkative creature continued to speak about the stadium. It wasn't much more than tidbits of information about things he had already told them—Loshar seemed to be talking mostly to fill the silence.

When they reached the command center, Loshar, true to his word, rummaged through a drawer for a moment and found Sividious an almanac. Like the program up in the stadium, the almanac was a thin square of flexible plastic about the size of a standard sheet of paper. The edges were dark but the center part glowed a soft green as holographic information flickered into existence.

"This one's a touch screen," Loshar told him, showing him how to manipulate the information with the tips of his fingers. "You can figure the time difference between any two locations by dragging them to this box here."

Jackie removed the guest pass lanyard Loshar had let her borrow and handed it to him. "Thanks again for the tour," she told him. "It was most interesting."

"*Olomosei tel'kamvarei tel poto,*" he said, but Jackie could only guess at the meaning.

"And thank you for the almanac," Sividious said, then he bowed politely, and he and Jackie started away.

"*Boko mala ine'we sa kolo,*" Loshar said, and Sividious called back, "We will." Then he and Jackie entered the corridor leading back to the Owners' Lounge, and the Jemkalat disappeared from view.

"What did he say?" Jackie asked.

"He said for us to come visit him again."

"Oh," she said then waited until they were safely out of earshot before speaking her next thought. It was a thought that had troubled her since the beginning of the tour. "What if Loshar looks up the world of Tatooine or the Yoda Galaxy in the astronomical almanac?"

"He won't find much," Sividious answered.

"Isn't that bad?"

"Maybe. I kind of get the feeling that not too many people around this place speak the truth about very many things."

"Even Loshar?"

Sividious shook his head. "Him we can trust—about the information he gave us during the tour anyway."

"Won't he be mad if he finds out you lied to him?"

"Perhaps. But I suspect he already knows I wasn't telling the truth about where we're from. He must not have been too offended by it, because he still took us on the tour."

"So where did you come up with my name?" she asked. "Albert Einstein, I know. But who is Marie Curie?"

"Another scientist," Sividious answered. "A chemist, actually. She discovered radium and polonium in the late eighteen hundreds. She received the Nobel Prize for it."

"Oh," she said then brushed the thought away. "So what do we do now?"

"We head back home to wait for Loshar's shift to end. We'll come back for Aya once he's gone."

"But Loshar said she won't be back for twenty-four hours."

"Right," Sividious agreed. "But that is only eight hours of Earth time." He checked his watch. "We've been here in the stadium for almost three hours," he told her. "Back on Earth only one hour will have passed. That means it's only about four thirty. We'll go home, do our homework, spend time with our families so they won't know we're up to something, and then when the eight hours are up, we'll come back for Aya."

"But that puts the return time right in the middle of the night for us."

Sividious nodded. "Pretty good time to sneak back up here, don't you think?"

"I suppose so," she said, but she wasn't so sure. "It might be better if we wait until after school tomorrow so we can come at the same time we did today."

Sividious stopped walking and pulled out the almanac. After fiddling with the screen for a moment, he smiled. "I think you might be on to something," he said. "According to this, a day in the stadium consists of thirty-six hours. That's twelve hours on Earth. So . . ." he fiddled with the almanac some more, "if we come back tomorrow at around the same time we came today, Loshar won't be here yet. If I figured this right, we would have about three hours to get Aya out before Loshar starts his shift."

"And why is it so important not to come while he is here?"

"Two reasons," Sividious said. "First: the other guard on duty won't recognize us. And second: I don't want Loshar to get in trouble. I kind of like the guy."

Jackie nodded. "Tomorrow it is." She looked around nervously. "Now, can we get out of here? I've had a little too much weirdness for one day."

Sividious put his arm around her, and they started walking again. "It is a bit overwhelming, isn't it?" he said.

"A *bit?*" she asked sarcastically. "I've never been so freaked out in my entire life."

Sividious laughed, and they continued down the corridor in silence.

18
BENEFICIAL AMBUSH

TROKAR LOMASEL'S REPTILIAN EYES GLOWED with satisfaction as he studied the information on the computer monitor in front of him. The All Access Pass that Aya the Kelsprite had stolen from him had returned to the stadium. Trokar had suspected it might be so—it was why he'd had the stadium's central computer do a trace on the AAP's serial number. Whoever Aya had given the AAP to obviously didn't know the stadium's central computer logged each and every time the passes were used. It was how he had known that Aya had fled to the primitive world of Portal T16.

He returned his attention to the green glow of the screen before him. Because of the central computer's ability to track individual passes, he had the complete record of the travels of whoever Aya had given the pass to. The person had experimented a bit at first, coming to the stadium for a brief visit—probably trying to decide if it was real or not—and then for a longer visit to watch Aya's competition with Shoar. The fool had even been brazen enough to use the pass to sit in reserved seating.

Trokar entered his password to access the security cameras and pulled up the footage from Level 1. Set to record whenever an event was held, the cameras—and there were thousands of them—captured the activities of the spectators as they moved about the various levels. That way, if a problem occurred, such as a fight or riot, the Agents could sort through what happened and punish those involved.

But the window for viewing footage was small since the amount of video captured was so vast it would quickly overwhelm the central computer if not deleted regularly. So unless a disturbance was reported, the video footage autodeleted four hours after every event. Fortunately they were still within the window.

He smiled as the footage of the mystery guest appeared on the screen. It showed a young male humanoid using the stolen AAP to access an elevator to the lower levels. He was dressed in the robes of a Chal'masa, and he wasn't alone. A young female, similarly dressed, was with him. Trokar felt a rush of surprise at the discovery, having anticipated only a single trespasser.

He watched on the various cameras as the two young humanoids exited the elevator into the Owners' Lounge and crossed to Section F of the Locker Rooms. The lack of hesitation showed they had known where Aya was being held. Whoever these two were, they were both knowledgeable and determined. And now their intent was obvious—they had come to free Aya.

And, Trokar thought with amusement, *they are still inside the stadium. Somewhere in the lower levels, searching for Aya.*

They wouldn't find her, of course. She was still in the medical facilities having her injuries attended to. Once again she had proven far more resourceful and dangerous than any of them had anticipated.

He shook his head in frustration. They needed to find a competitor who could defeat her before she won the Jomon Tournament and achieved Free Agent status. Because if she won, she would undoubtedly use her new status to leave the Games and return to her homeworld. And that would severely hinder recruiting on that world for years to come. Maybe even forever.

Frowning, Trokar downloaded the information into his handheld, pulled the miniature computer from its port, and rose to his feet. After activating the handheld's ability for wireless communication with the central computer, he set it to notify him the next time the stolen AAP was used. This would allow him to track the intruder anywhere in the stadium in real time. Not that it really mattered—he already knew where they were from. If he wanted, he could simply wait for them at the entrance of Portal T16 and capture them there.

But Trokar didn't like to wait for his prey to come to him. He liked to hunt. He would meet the would-be rescuers in the lower levels. He had no doubt they would retrace their path. He would intercept them when they did.

The thought made him smile. And then he would toss them into the arena to become a snack for a creature like Shoar the Dragon Centipede. Their deaths would make for a fine pregame show.

Still smiling, he clipped his zobo stick to his belt, pulled out his laser pistol to check the power level, then returned the weapon to the holster, and adjusted his trench coat. He didn't expect much of a fight from beings from a world as primitive as T16, but it was best not to take any chances.

As he started for the corridor that would take him to a docking station for the pneumatic railcars, he momentarily considered calling for backup, then decided he'd rather handle this himself. It added excitement to the hunt. Even more important, doing this alone would elevate his status among the Kaladan Secret Police and earn him a long-overdue promotion.

His decision made, he climbed into one of the slender, bullet-shaped vehicles and pressed the button that sent him hurtling through the bowels of the stadium in a rush of silent wind. His hunt for Aya's would-be rescuers had begun.

* * *

The energy shield deactivated at their approach, and Sividious and Jackie passed into the Owners' Lounge and crossed to the elevator without speaking. The various beings in the room glanced at them as they entered then quickly averted their eyes when they spotted the Chal'masa robes. Sividious smiled inwardly. He never would have guessed that such simple attire could inspire so much fear.

He and Jackie reached the elevator, but the doors didn't open at their approach. There were no buttons to push either, just a square of black plastic about ten inches wide. The soft glow of red beneath the surface of the plastic hinted at a laser scanner.

Leaning forward, Sividious removed the AAP from inside his robes and held it up to the scanner. As expected, there was a flicker of red as the AAP was scanned, then the doors opened with a mechanical hiss.

"After you, Madam Curie," he said to Jackie then followed her inside. He looked at the rows of buttons, pushed the one for Level 16, and leaned back against the wall. The doors closed, and they were on their way.

"I'm going to be soooo glad to get out of here," Jackie said at last, and Sividious nodded.

"I'll be glad when we never have to come back," he told her.

"I've been wondering about that," she said then held up her hand as she clarified, "not about coming back for Aya—that we *have* to do. I mean after we've freed her." She hesitated. "I mean, are you really going to turn your back on this place and never return? I know you, Sividious. You love science too much to simply forget about all of this."

Sividious shrugged. "I like to live too," he told her. "And I have no doubt that messing around in here too much will draw the kind of attention that will get me killed."

She raised an eyebrow at him, and he smiled.

"But I won't deny that I am tempted," he added. "Very tempted. I'm just not crazy."

She laughed. "That's debatable."

Sividious felt the elevator slow, then the doors opened and he found himself staring into the reptilian eyes of a Kaladan Agent. The creature's slitted pupils glimmered with mirth as he took them in, and his mouth broke into a jagged-toothed smile. His posture, along with the amusement on his face, told Sividious he had been expecting them.

The Agent looked from him to Jackie then back to him. "You are not Chal'masa," he hissed disdainfully. He reached for the baton at his waist, and the deadly weapon crackled to life with sizzling blue energy.

Sividious brought his cattle prod up to defend himself, but the Agent knocked it away in a shower of sparks. The burst of energy from the baton was so powerful it numbed Sividious's hands and caused the prod's battery pack to explode.

The explosion rocked the interior of the elevator, and Sividious was nearly knocked from his feet. Blinking against the flash of light and plume of acrid smoke, he looked up to find the Agent looming over him.

Yellow eyes glowing, the fish-faced creature raised the baton to strike him but gave a surprised hiss as Jackie used one of her karate moves to kick his feet out from under him.

The Agent landed heavily on his back, and the air blasted from his lungs. He lost his grip on the baton, and the weapon's energy vanished as the baton clattered noisily to the floor. Snarling in anger, the Agent reached for the gun at his hip then howled in pain as Jackie jabbed the would-be gun hand with her cattle prod. The Agent tried to bat the prod away with his other hand, but Jackie kicked the creature hard in the ribs. Then, before the Agent could move farther, she jabbed the cattle prod against his neck and pulled the trigger.

Howling, the Agent jerked and jolted as nine thousand volts of pure shock racked his body, robbing it of strength and stripping it of mobility. When Jackie finally pulled the cattle prod away, the Kaladan Agent went as limp as a rag.

"Good work," Sividious said, trying to shake the numbness from his hands. When Jackie didn't respond, he turned to look at her. Her eyes were wide, and she looked on the verge of tears. She stared at the unconscious Agent as if she couldn't believe what she had just done.

Sividious took her arm and made her look at him. "You did good, Jackie," he told her. "You just saved both our lives."

She blinked at him. "I didn't even know what I was doing," she admitted. "I saw him attack you and my reflexes just took over. What is that thing? I didn't kill him, did I?" She actually sounded worried that she had.

"It would have been a good thing if you did," he answered. "But, no, he's still alive. As for what it is—" He shook his head in disgust. "It's a Kaladan Agent. And I'd say he was looking for us. Waiting for us, actually. Somehow the thing knew we were coming this way."

"How?"

"I don't know," Sividious said. "But I intend to find out. Here, help me strip him of his weapons and stuff. If he starts to come to, hit him with the cattle prod again."

"Actually," she said, moving to retrieve the fallen baton, "I'd rather use this." She pressed a button and it crackled to life. She took up a position above the Agent and motioned for Sividious to continue.

Sividious quickly removed the Agent's gun, his AAP, and a small handheld computer. He touched the screen to activate it, then blinked in surprise at the amount of information it contained. He scanned it for a few moments, using the touch-screen to scroll through the different menus and databases, then shook his head in awe.

"That looks like a smartphone," Jackie said.

"Oh, it's much more than that," Sividious told her, showing her the screen. "The Agent used it to track us. Apparently the stadium has a central computer that logs every use of an AAP. Not the little insignificant ones with restricted access, just those with enough clearance to compromise the stadium. But there are still thousands of them." He frowned at the next bit of information. "And each pass has a serial number that can be traced. He must have known which AAP Aya stole— he used the serial number to track us down. It's all here, every shield we deactivated, every restricted area we entered."

"So he probably knows we were trying to help Aya," Jackie said, sounding like she wanted to smack the Agent with the baton.

"Looks like it," Sividious said, scrolling through the handheld's menu. He found what he was looking for and entered the serial number of the Agent's AAP into the window that would activate the tracking program. He thought it strange that the Agent had come alone when he could have easily brought an entire army of Agents with him, and he wanted to know where the creature had been and if he had spoken to other Agents or activated any kind of alarm system.

"According to this log," Sividious told her, "no alarm has been sounded, and it doesn't appear as if the Agent spoke to anyone else. If he had, we would have been captured for sure."

"What else is on that thing?" she asked.

He grinned at her. "Everything," he said, continuing to work his way through the menus. "Work schedules for employees like Loshar, schedules for events and tournaments, the names of all the participants (both Draftees and Free Agents), the names of Owners, you name it—Hello!" he said, cutting off in surprise.

"What is it?" Jackie asked.

"The entire schematic blueprint for the stadium," he told her, excitement washing through him in waves.

"You mean like a map?"

"Not just a map," he told her. "*The* map. We can find our way through any part of the stadium with this thing."

19
FROM CAPTOR TO CAPTIVE

Jackie found Sividious's excitement regarding his newfound toy amusing, but right now she thought they had more important things to consider. She looked down at their prisoner. "So what do we do with him?" she asked, poking the Agent with her toe. He was still unconscious, but there was no telling how long that might last. "We can't kill him," she added, "no matter how evil or unhuman-like he might be."

Sividious studied the Agent for a moment without speaking, his eyes intense, his lips pursed in that tight way that showed he was thinking. Finally, he said, "We exile him. We take him through a portal and leave him in the world beyond." He fiddled with the handheld for a moment, and his face registered a smile. "And I know just the place. Come on, help me drag him." He took one of the Agent's feet and waited for Jackie to take the other.

"Where are we taking him?" she grunted as she started pulling. The Agent was heavier than she had thought he would be, so she deactivated the baton and tucked it under her arm so she could use both hands.

"Portal P16 is one of many that are shielded," he said. "According to the information in the handheld, the world beyond is under lockdown due to a war. The Kaladan have suspended recruiting from that world indefinitely." He grinned. "But the best part is, the world is dominated by magic, not technology. Without his AAP, and with no way to contact his buddies here in the stadium, there will be no way he can return. He'll be stranded there."

"But what about when the war ends and recruiting starts up again? He might find a way to return then."

He shrugged. "By then we will have finished what we came here to do. And trust me, once this is over, I never want to come back."

As they neared Portal P16, the energy shield deactivated in response to the AAP. They stopped short of entering the corridor beyond, and Sividious turned to face her. "I want you to wait here," he told her, but she shook her head, angry that he would even suggest such a thing.

"No, Siv. I'm coming with you."

"Not this time," he barked, and she flinched at the harshness in his voice.

He held up a hand. "I'm sorry," he said, his voice much softer than before. "I didn't mean to yell. But this world is off-limits for a reason. It will be dangerous there, and I—" He cut off, looking away in embarrassment as his cheeks flushed red. "I can't risk that something might happen to you."

Jackie didn't know how to respond. The feminist in her wanted to punch him in the face for being a pigheaded chauvinist boy, but the romantic in her wanted to hug him for his chivalry. That he was scared for her was obvious. That there might be a good reason for such fear was just as clear.

Finally, she nodded. "Fine. I'll wait here. But if you aren't back in ten minutes, I'm coming after you. So give me one of the AAPs."

Smiling with what could only be relief, Sividious handed over the AAP he'd taken from the Agent. He started to hand her the Agent's gun, but she shook her head.

"You keep that," she told him. "If this world is as dangerous as you say, you might need it. In fact," she added, "you might need this as well." She handed him the baton.

He belted the gun around his waist then clipped on the baton. Taking the Agent by the feet, he dragged him into the narrow corridor leading to the portal. The energy shield sprang back into place as soon as he was inside, and Jackie was forced to watch through the shimmering blue as Sividious and his captive receded into the darkening distance. She waited for the flash of white that was Sividious passing through into the world beyond, then moved to a bench near a concession stand and sat down to wait.

* * *

The world into which Sividious arrived with the unconscious Agent was not at all like he had expected it to be. The handheld had shown a bright, vibrant world covered with lush forests and filled with all manner of life—beautiful humanoids of varying races and magical creatures of every shape and size.

What he found was a pale, sickly world of wilt and decay. The sky was shrouded with low-hanging clouds, and the air was pungent and caused him to wrinkle his nose in disgust. There was no sign of life anywhere. No movement. No sound. It was as if the world itself had died.

Confused, Sividious pulled out the handheld to investigate the discrepancy, thumbing through the menus until he found the profile of Portal P16. It showed the same beautiful images as before, but when he scrolled to the bottom of the profile, he discovered that the images had been taken before the war had started. And now the war was over.

There had been no winner.

Sividious continued to scroll through the information at the bottom of the page and was horrified to discover that the desolation spreading before him was the aftermath of an attack of magic so terrible and so powerful it had destroyed the entire world.

Even more horrifying was how the destruction had altered the passage of time in this world. Where before the ratio between here and the stadium had been nearly identical—one minute for one minute—now it stood at one minute for one hour.

He looked at the arch that marked this side of the portal, and his heart nearly stopped in his chest. Jackie should have joined him by now, he realized. If what he'd just read about the time difference was true, she should have grown bored with waiting and should have come in search of him like she said she would.

Leaving the Kaladan Agent to its fate in the ruined world, Sividious drew the stolen gun from its holster and raced back through the portal. If anything had happened to Jackie . . .

* * *

When Sividious didn't return after the allotted ten minutes, Jackie began to grow uneasy. *I should have gone with him,* she thought darkly.

Rising from the bench, she crossed to the portal entrance, but the energy shield didn't deactivate at her approach. Startled, she stared at it in confusion for a moment then pulled out the All Access Pass and waved it in front of the scanner.

Nothing happened.

She took a closer look at the AAP, and her heart sank when she discovered that the internal circuitry had been fried. *It must have been the cattle prod,* she thought as she shook her head in disgust. She should have tested the AAP before Sividious left.

She looked around nervously, suddenly aware of how vulnerable she was if someone should come along. She was alone with a broken—not to mention *stolen*—AAP, a ruined cattle prod, a prod with only half a charge, and a tube of pepper spray. She had no way to communicate with anyone she might meet, and she really didn't want to have to try. Most of the beings she'd seen so far gave her the heebie-jeebies. Most of them looked like they could kill her with very little effort and without the least bit of remorse.

Well, this stinks, she thought, moving away from the shimmering wall of blue energy to the darkness of an enclave near a bank of computers. Once there, she tossed the ruined AAP into one of the garbage incinerators she'd seen the spectators using then tossed the ruined cattle prod in after it. Shaking her head in disgust, she hunkered down in the shadows to wait for Sividious to return. She had no idea what was taking him so long.

A short time later, voices sounded from somewhere down the corridor. They grew louder as the speakers drew near, and Jackie pressed herself deeper into the shadows and went still.

Three shapes came into view, moving casually as they spoke to one another in a harsh, guttural language. Each wore a trench coat and carried an energy baton.

Agents! she thought and held her breath as they moved past. She offered a quick prayer that they wouldn't look her way.

They were just about out of view when one of the Agents suddenly stopped and sniffed the air, muttering to the others. Those two stopped as well and began sniffing the air. One of them hissed, and the darkness of the corridor was suddenly awash in the blue light of their energy wands.

Jackie remained still, but it didn't matter. They had already seen her. The one who had stopped first motioned toward her with his baton and snarled something in his language. She had no idea how the creatures could see anything with those sunglasses on, but apparently they could.

When she didn't move, he snarled again and his baton flared brightly.

A heartbeat later, a burst of blue energy struck her, and the world flashed into darkness.

20
A NEW MISSION

THE CORRIDOR IN FRONT OF Portal P16 was as quiet as a tomb, and Sividious looked about warily as he softly called Jackie's name. She should have been right here, or at least within earshot, to meet him when he returned. But there was no sign of her anywhere. That meant one of two things: she'd either gotten bored during the three plus hours she was alone here and had gone exploring, or she had been discovered by some undesirable creature.

He ruled the first option out immediately—she would have joined him in the portal if she had grown bored of waiting. That meant something had chased her off. Or worse yet, had captured her.

He holstered the gun and moved into the shadows where banks of computers protruded from the wall. He powered one on, then took the Agent's smartphone-looking device and plugged it into the computer's docking port. He knew the handheld had wireless capability, but the signal had been lost when he'd left the stadium. A little red dial in one corner of the screen showed it was logging back in.

A beep sounded, and the red dial turned green. He was in the system. Now all he had to do was find out what had happened to Jackie. But where to look? He didn't have the serial number for her AAP, so he couldn't initiate a trace on it. Instead, he found the menu for the stadium's video surveillance system and pulled up the cameras stationed around Portal P16.

Another dead end. The cameras were only active during events, and the footage ended shortly after all the spectators had exited the stadium. But even that was no longer available because the stadium's central processing unit autodeleted footage after four hours.

Where in the heck did she go?

A thought struck him, and a cold pit of dread settled in his stomach. Scrolling through the menus, he found the roster for the Locker Rooms and pulled up the most recent entries. One in particular caught his eye.

Recruit 4895PJR667LK
Locker: SL5-B6-38L
Name: Unknown
Species: Humanoid
Homeworld: Unknown
Gender: Female
Age: Undetermined
Height: 5'4"
Weight: 115 lbs
Assignment: Romasar Tournament Pregame
Opponent: Gordorian Firetoads

Jackie, he thought. *It has to be.*

He downloaded the information into the handheld, then pulled it from the port and powered down the computer. Moving to the edge of the corridor, he looked in each direction as he tried to decide what to do next.

Knowing where Jackie was being held was one thing—getting to her without being seen was something else altogether. The upper levels of the stadium might be empty in between events, but the lower levels likely never shut down. Even with the Agent's handheld to guide him, chances were he would run into someone or something.

And yet he had to try. Jackie would certainly do as much for him.

He wondered briefly if he should go back to Earth and get help—Sam maybe, or Jackie's brother Caleb—but he shook the thought away. There wasn't enough time even if he could convince them that he wasn't crazy.

Activating the handheld, he pulled up the events schedule and found that the Romasar Tournament was set to start in a little over an hour. Not a lot of time considering that the Kaladan would probably take her from her cell long before the tournament started so they could move her to the playing fiel—

That's it! he thought excitedly. *That's how I'll get her out!*

It was crazy, of course, but it was so crazy it might actually work. All he needed now was a trench coat and a pair of sunglasses.

* * *

When Jackie came to, she found herself strapped to a chair in the center of a small room. Her arms were free from the elbows down, but her upper arms were clamped tight against her body by metal bands. When she tried to move her feet, she felt metal bands around her ankles.

A single bright light burned overhead, shining in her face and making it difficult to see much farther than her knees. Dark shapes moving beyond the edge of the light told her she wasn't alone. *Agents,* she thought with dread, *or worse.*

A harsh voice muttered something unintelligible, and one of the dark shapes—it was indeed an Agent—stepped into the light and placed a metal ring on top of her head, fitting a small speaker up to her ear.

"Who are you?" the fish-faced creature asked. "What world are you from?"

Jackie knew better than to answer, so she stared at him as if she didn't understand what he was saying. It was a look she had perfected in math class.

The Agent slapped her hard across the face, stinging her cheek and making specks of light dance beneath her eyelids. It also knocked the metal ring from her head. Snarling, the Agent retrieved it and fitted the speaker back up to her ear.

"I said, who are you, and where are you from?" He raised his hand as if he might strike her again and waited.

Jackie glared at him but said nothing. Nor did she flinch when he tensed as if he were going to hit her. When he didn't, Jackie decided it was because he didn't want to have to pick up the earpiece again and not because he wouldn't enjoy hurting her. She could see in his snake-like eyes that causing pain was something he enjoyed.

"Maybe she speaks a language not yet entered into the system," another Agent said from beyond the light. "It wouldn't be the first time a life-form from an uncharted system found its way here."

"Yes," a voice behind her said. "It's possible she escaped during the Heishari fireworks explosion on Sublevel 12."

"The one caused by the Gordorian Firetoad?" the first Agent asked. He sounded skeptical.

"Yes. The fireworks belonged to the Thelemon Trading Company, but it wasn't the only merchandise involved in the accident. The Holishar Empire lost eight Recruits as well. Only five have been accounted for. Their bodies were found in the wreckage."

"The other three could have been vaporized in the explosion," the Agent looming over Jackie countered.

"Or they could have escaped in the chaos," the Agent behind her offered.

The first Agent shook his head. "I refuse to believe a creature as pathetic as this could have made it to Level 16 without anyone noticing."

Jackie's heart burned with anger, but she remained still and continued to pretend like she didn't understand a word they were saying.

The Agents fell silent as they studied her. After what seemed an eternity, the first one spoke. "If she was part of the Holishar Empire's Recruits, it would explain her inability to understand us. The Holishar Space Pirates are famous for their escapades into uncharted systems. They pride themselves on finding new life-forms to bring to the Games. Her language must not yet be uploaded into the central computer."

"So what do we do with her?" the Agent behind her asked.

Terrified though she was about what the answer might be, Jackie kept her face unreadable as she waited for the first Agent to speak.

"We put her in the Romasar Pregame Show," he said with an evil laugh. "We'll let the Gordorian Firetoads finish what they started."

* * *

With a hiss of automated pistons, the door of the pneumatic railcar opened, and Sividious climbed out into the darkness of the docking station in Section B of Sublevel 5. He adjusted the trench coat and hat he'd stolen from a supply closet the handheld had directed him to on Sublevel 3, then he pulled out the pair of sunglasses he'd taken from the same closet.

He studied them for a moment, unsure about wearing them. How was he supposed to see his way through the dark places in the stadium with sunglasses on? He'd probably trip over something and give himself away as an imposter the first dark place he entered.

And yet the Kaladan seemed able to wear them in the dark just fine. Maybe their reptilian eyes were better suited to the darkness than his human eyes. Or maybe . . .

He put the sunglasses on, and the dim interior of the docking station came into luminescent view as video screens built into the lenses activated in front of his eyes. It was the best night-vision technology he had ever seen. In fact, it didn't look like night vision at all—it looked more like a movie in HD on a plasma screen television.

Cool!

He couldn't believe his luck in finding the closet, especially since the discovery had resulted in more than just a new disguise. Reaching into his coat pocket, he withdrew the zobo stick—he'd learned the name from the handheld—and clipped it next to the gun on the belt at his waist. He hoped he wouldn't have to use either of the weapons, but he would if it meant getting Jackie out of here alive.

Leaving the docking station behind, he started down the narrow corridor that would take him to the Owners' Lounge, which fronted the Locker Rooms where Jackie was being held. He knew various beings would be in the lounge, but he trusted his disguise would encourage them to mind their own business. The maintenance workers on Sublevel 3 had certainly looked the other way as he'd passed through the generator room they were repairing. It should work here too.

The energy shield deactivated as he neared, and Sividious moved into the Lounge without hesitation. A sudden hush fell over the room as the dozen or so beings inside spotted him, and every single one of them stopped what they were doing to watch him pass. The zobo stick on his waist drew most of the attention, which was fine with him—it meant they weren't looking too closely at his face.

He passed through into the corridor beyond and breathed a sigh of relief when the energy shield sprang into place behind him. So far so good. Now all he had to do was make it past whoever or whatever was on duty at the Locker Room's control center.

The shimmering wall of blue faded at his approach, and he strode into the large octagonal room beyond. With barely a glance at the werewolf-like creature seated in the raised control center, Sividious started for the third corridor on his left. He was just about there when the wolf-thing called to him.

"Can I help you, Officer Agent, sir?" he asked.

"No," Sividious growled without turning or stopping. He hoped the nasty reputation of the Kaladan Agents would be enough to keep the creature from inquiring further.

It was, and he continued on without incident.

When he reached cell 38L, he shot a quick glance in each direction, then used his AAP to deactivate the shield.

21
JAILBREAK

CLUTCHING HER KNEES TO HER chest with both arms, Jackie huddled in the corner of her cell and tried to stop crying. It was the third attempt in as many minutes, and so far she hadn't been successful. Her cheeks glistened in the light of the energy shield filling the door.

She hated crying because of the gender stereotype she always associated with the tears, but right now she couldn't help it. She was scared, and her body ached from being shot with the baton and from the rough treatment she'd received from the Agents in the interrogation room.

The thought of how they'd treated her made her angry, and just like that the tears stopped. She wiped her cheeks with the sleeve of her karate robe then took a deep breath to steady her nerves. *Focus on the anger,* she told herself. *Anger is better than fear.*

She rose to her feet and moved to peer out through the energy shield. The corridor appeared empty, but she couldn't see very far in either direction, so she had no way of knowing if she was truly alone or if the Agents had posted a guard. She didn't know why they would have; the energy shield was more than enough to keep her from leaving.

She spit at the shimmering field and was rewarded with a loud sizzle as her spit vaporized in an angry flash.

"Stupid shield," she muttered then moved to the slender shelf-like bench that slid from the wall at her approach. The only "furniture" in the room, it was probably meant to serve as a bed, though she didn't imagine it would be a whole lot more comfortable than sleeping on the floor.

She exhaled in disgust, fully immersing herself in her anger as she contemplated what she would do next. She only had a couple of options. One was to wait for Sividious to rescue her—an event she didn't think all that likely even with his being such a genius with all this technological crap—the other was to take out another Agent with her martial arts skills.

She frowned. This time she would use his own weapon on him. And she wouldn't stop until the filthy creature was dead.

A few hours ago the thought of killing another being would have made her sick. Now she realized how naive she had been. The Kaladan fully intended to kill her for the sake of their twisted Games; she must be willing to do the same in order to survive.

An Agent stopped in front of her cell, and her heart skipped a beat when she realized that her opportunity for escape had come much sooner than she had anticipated. All she had to do now was take him out with a karate move and get his baton away from him. After that . . .

The shield deactivated, and Jackie readied a kick as the Agent stepped into the room.

"Jackie?" a voice whispered.

Sividious.

She relaxed her stance, her anger vanishing beneath a wave of relief and gratitude. She should have known Sividious would come for her. She shouldn't have doubted his ability to find her. And yet she couldn't get all mushy right now either. She needed him to believe that she had been strong in his absence.

The sight of him standing there in the door of her cellblock dressed as an Agent and armed to the teeth with technologically superior weapons made her think of Luke Skywalker.

She grinned at him. "Aren't you a little short for a Stormtrooper?" she asked, doing her best Princess Leia impersonation. She even put her hand on her hip and tilted her head skeptically.

"Very funny," he muttered as he removed the sunglasses. His face softened as he looked her over carefully. "Are you all right?"

"I'm a little sore from being shot with one of those batons," she told him. "And my cheek hurts from where one of the Agents slapped me during my interrogation. But I'm all right enough to kick their trash if we run into any more of them. I was just getting ready to kick yours because I thought you were an Agent."

"Atta girl," Sividious said. Reaching into his trench coat, he pulled out a second baton and handed it to her. "It's called a zobo stick. You already know that the bottom button activates the wand function. The top button is what shoots a burst. On its highest setting, it's lethal. I've got ours set for stun. I had a feeling you would be in the mood to thrash somebody, and I would rather we don't kill anything on our way out. It might make coming back for Aya that much more difficult."

Jackie tapped her palm with the zobo stick. "Why don't we just go get her right now?"

"Because she probably isn't back yet," he answered. "Even if she is, I don't want to get Loshar in trouble."

Jackie felt her anger rise. "Who cares if he gets in trouble," she growled. "He's a prison guard, for Pete's sake. One who works for the Kaladan. In my book that makes him as rotten as an Agent."

"Maybe, maybe not," Sividious said. "I got the feeling from some of the things he said that he might not have much say in the matter. He might be as much a slave to his 'assignment' as a guard as the recruits are to their assignments as players in the Games."

Jackie glared at him for a moment then took a deep breath and forced herself to relax. "I'm sorry," she said. "I'm not mad at you. I'm mad at the Kaladan, their Agents, and this whole stupid stadium."

Sividious smiled. "I know. That's why I set your zobo stick to stun."

She looked at him. "Am I really that predictable?"

"You are when you're mad," he said, then pulled a lanyard from his pocket and handed it to her. "It's a lesser grade Access Pass than the one I have," he told her, "but it will let you understand what others are saying. I stole it from a supply closet on my way to a pneumatic railcar terminal."

"A what?"

"You'll see," he said, putting the sunglasses back on and moving to the door. "Come on, let's get out of here."

"How can you see where you are going?" she asked as she moved up beside him and peeked out into the dark corridor.

"The sunglasses have night-vision capabil—" He cut off with an angry, "Crap!"

Jackie took his hand. "What's wrong?"

"The prison guard is coming down the corridor," he told her. "He probably saw on his computer that the shield for your cell had been deactivated."

"What are we going to do?"

"We're going to hope my disguise works," he answered. "Hide your zobo stick. I'm going to try to convince him that I'm taking you in for more questioning."

"And if that doesn't work?"

Sividious's face darkened. "Shoot him."

Jackie nodded. "With pleasure."

She watched the guard draw near and was creeped out by how much it looked like a werewolf. *A werewolf wearing battle fatigues and body armor,* she thought darkly. Apparently, the creature took his job way more seriously than Loshar did. The Jemkalat hadn't worn much more than a loincloth and his lanyard.

Or maybe, she corrected as she eyed the creature further, this wolf-thing stemmed from a world far more warlike and violent than Loshar's and was used to combat. If so, then he was decidedly more dangerous than she or Sividious had figured. Reaching inside her karate robe, she took hold of the zobo stick and placed her finger on the activation button. If the guard so much as looked at her funny, she would knock him into the next universe.

"Mr. Agent, sir," the wolf-guard said. "Please explain yourself." In spite of the obvious attempt to be polite, he sounded angry. "This prisoner isn't scheduled for release to the Games for another half hour. And I was told that the Agents who brought her in would be returning to collect her."

"There has been a change in plan," Sividious told him, making his voice rough. "This one needs further questioning."

The werewolf's eyes narrowed. "You will forgive me for saying so, but that is highly unusual. What could you possibly hope to learn from her that the others couldn't?" One of the guard's hands moved toward the pistol resting at his hip. It was a subtle movement, but it told Jackie the creature knew something was wrong.

If Sividious noticed, he didn't show it. "You dare question me?" he growled. "Out of my way, vermin, lest I assign you to the Games in this creature's stead."

The guard's eyes widened in surprise then narrowed in anger just as quickly. His lips curled into a silent sneer, showing two rows of glistening white fangs. The hair on his arms and neck bristled as he reached for his gun.

Panicked, Jackie sent the creature spinning into the wall with a burst of energy from her zobo stick. He struck the wall with a thud, slumped into a heap, and lay still. Jackie stared at him for a moment, wondering if she had killed him and deciding that she didn't really care if she had. It was an awful thought, she knew, but she couldn't help the way she felt.

Sividious turned to look at her. "Nice shot," he said. "How does it feel to be on the giving end of a zobo stick?"

"A lot better than it does to be on the receiving end," she told him. "Trust me, that dude is going to be sore in the morning."

"If he wakes up at all," Sividious said as he knelt next to the creature. "He hit his head pretty hard."

"Don't tell me you feel sorry for him," she scoffed.

"Sort of," he admitted. "Until we know more about the relationship these creatures have with their Kaladan masters, I'm inclined to believe they might not all be bad."

"This one was," Jackie told him. "He would have killed you if I hadn't shot him."

"I suppose so," Sividious said, taking the creature by his feet. "Here, take his gun and help me drag him back to the command center. If he doesn't die before the Agents return, they'll probably send him to the medical facilities to be treated."

"Yeah," Jackie muttered sarcastically as she stuck the gun inside her karate robe. "They'll want him nice and healthy before they interrogate him. Poor bugger," she added. "It might be better for him if we just finish him off."

Sividious stared at her in shock.

"I'm kidding," she said. "I would never harm a defenseless creature." She wrinkled her nose as she took one of the guard's feet to help Sividious. "No matter how bad he smells."

"Yeah, well, be careful with the gun. It fires beams of laser energy strong enough to blow the armor off a Dragon Centipede. So don't use it unless you have to. It makes a mess of anything it hits."

"And you know this because . . . ?"

"I tested mine on a crate in the closet I stole the trench coat and stuff from," he said. "There wasn't much left of the crate or its contents."

"Sweet."

Sividious shook his head at her. "Come on," he said. "We need to get out of here before the Agents who captured you come back or before someone else sees us." He flashed a dark smile. "Or before you decide to shoot something else."

22
LEAVE NO TRACE

DRAGGING THE UNCONSCIOUS GUARD, SIVIDIOUS and Jackie moved down the narrow corridor of the cellblock and into the command center. The large octagonal room was quiet save for the hum of computers and the soft rush of air from a ventilation duct. The rows of lights on the guard's main control panel were green, showing that no alarm had been sounded.

Motioning for Jackie to wait where she was, Sividious climbed the ladder to the control panel then took out the stolen handheld and plugged it into the command center's main computer. It was time to find out if an Agent's security clearance was as high as he suspected. If so, he was about to create a distraction that would keep the rest of the Agents busy for the next several hours.

The light on the handheld turned green, and the cellblock's main menu flickered to life on the screen in front of him. He pulled up the screen that controlled the power levels of each of the cellblock's two hundred energy shields, then he scrolled down to the small window framing the cutoff switch that would kill power to the entire lot. *I hope this works,* he thought as he tapped the big red button with his finger. The electric hum filling each of the corridors faded to silence.

Pleased with himself, he exited the cellblock's computer, turned to smile at Jackie—and found a robot descending from a hidden compartment in the high, domed ceiling.

Shaped like a football helmet, it was roughly the size of a basketball and floated several feet above the floor. It had a single blue line for an eye and a pair of arms tipped with metal prongs. The arms, Sividious realized, looked an awful lot like zobo sticks. When the prongs crackled to life with blue energy, he knew he had been right. He should have known there would be a backup system. Obviously, this robot was the mechanized form of an Agent.

Its blue gaze settled on Sividious. "Identify yourself," the robot demanded, its metallic voice actually managing to sound angry.

"I'm an Agent, you fool!" Sividious snapped, huffing himself up grandly. He didn't know if the robot could be intimidated, but it was worth a try.

"Invalid identification," the robot replied, and the ends of its pronged arms flared brightly as it readied a strike.

A nanosecond later it exploded into thousands of molten scraps that rained across the command center like a miniature meteor shower, trailing sparks and filling the air with acrid smoke.

Startled, Sividious turned to find Jackie looking down the sights of the laser pistol she'd taken from the unconscious prison guard. She looked as surprised as he did by the extent of the destruction the pistol had wrought upon the robot.

Sividious jumped down from the raised command center and crossed to where she was staring at the gun in awe.

"Thanks for saving me," he told her. "That thing would have killed me." He glanced at the smoldering shards scattered across the room then turned his attention to movement visible down some of the corridors. The sound of voices, both organic and metallic, was growing louder, and flashes of blue showed that other prison robots were working to subdue the escapees.

"What did you do?" Jackie asked, peering past him at the quickly growing chaos in the cellblocks.

"Covered our trail, I hope," he told her then flinched as a burst of blue energy sizzled past his head. It slammed into the wall in a spray of color that dissipated along the metal in crackling flashes.

Pushing him aside, Jackie raised the laser pistol and shot another robot as it emerged from one of the corridors. Like the first, it exploded into flaming shards and a plume of smoke.

"Time to go," Sividious said, taking her by the arm and turning her toward the shielded doorway leading to the Owners' Lounge. "By the time the Agents fix this mess," he continued, "they'll have no idea who was responsible for it."

She nodded her understanding. "If I had been the only prisoner to come up missing . . ."

"They would have blamed you. And they would have known you had help." He smiled, extremely pleased with himself. "This way they'll probably never know the truth."

"Won't the guard tell them what happened?"

Sividious shrugged. "He'll try. But I don't think his story will be very credible in light of how incompetent he is as a prison guard. If he's smart, he'll slip off to his homeworld and disappear before the Kaladan decide what to do with him."

Jackie shook her head. "And you thought I was being cruel by wanting to kill him," she muttered.

They were nearly to the Owners' Lounge when Jackie suddenly stopped and grabbed his arm. "Wait a second," she said, sounding worried. "I thought you said the stadium's central computer tracked each and every use of an AAP. If that is true, then the Agents are going to know that someone let me out. And they will also know that someone killed the power on all the doors and let everyone else out too."

Sividious made a calming motion with his hand. "Already thought of that," he told her then started her walking again. "It's why we need to hurry up to Level 16. There's a computer terminal near our portal that I can use to erase all records concerning this particular AAP. But I need to do it before other Agents start searching the database to try to get a handle on what happened here."

"Oh," Jackie said. "Well, let's hurry, then."

He pointed at the zobo stick she carried. "Hide that inside your robe while we pass through the Owners' Lounge," he told her. "And try to look scared. You are supposed to be my prisoner, after all."

"That won't be hard," she told him. "I'm totally freaked right now."

"Me too," he admitted. "Lucky for me I have these glasses." He motioned her forward. "After you, madam prisoner."

The beings in the lounge looked up as he and Jackie entered then quickly found something else to occupy their attention when they spotted the trench coat and zobo stick. Safe behind the enhanced vision of the sunglasses, he watched them closely anyway. He was nervous that they would see through the disguise, and he wanted to be ready to stop them if they decided to raise an alarm. But the assortment of creatures kept their heads down and their eyes averted, and he and Jackie moved into the corridor leading to the pneumatic railcars without incident. Ten seconds later they were speeding through the interior of the stadium in a rush of wind.

"So far so good," Jackie whispered as she gazed out the viewport at the stream of lights whizzing past.

"So far," Sividious agreed, but he wasn't going to relax until he was back in his own world. There were still too many things that could go wrong. It would only take one Agent seeing them for all heck to break loose. If he and Jackie were forced to fight their way out of the stadium, it would destroy all chances of them coming back for Aya. It might even make the Kaladan reconsider their belief that the primitive world of Portal T16 wasn't worth exploiting. He and Jackie might very well be endangering the entire human race.

The interior of the pneumatic car rotated within its casing as the bullet-shaped vehicle began the steep climb to the upper levels, and Sividious smiled when he saw the surprised look on Jackie's face.

"It keeps the passengers level," he explained. "That makes it possible to have both horizontal and vertical travel with the same vehicle." He pointed to the string of lights streaking down the center of the viewport, where only moments before they had been streaking across it.

"So it's a Wonkavator," Jackie said.

"A what?"

"A Wonkavator," she repeated. "You know, like in *Willy Wonka and the Chocolate Factory.*"

"Sure," Sividious agreed. "Only this one won't shoot us out through the roof." He readied himself as the car came to a stop. "We're here," he said, stating the obvious. "I'll go first to make sure the way is clear, but have your gun ready just in case. Don't use it unless you have to."

She put on an air of innocence. "Who me?"

He ignored the sarcasm. "We are about ten portals away from T16, so we are going to have to walk."

He hit the button to open the door, which vanished into the interior of the car with a lightning-fast hiss. Tightening his grip on the zobo stick, he stepped out into the darkened chamber beyond, took a quick look around, then motioned for Jackie to join him. He pointed to the energy shield at the opposite end of the room.

"The main corridor is just beyond that door," he told her. "Portal T16 will be to the right. The Romasar Tournament is set to start in less than thirty minutes, so it's possible that spectators will have started to arrive. If nothing else, the vendors will already be setting up. I'll go first, and then you come about thirty seconds later. That way if anyone sees us they won't know we are together. An Agent walking alone isn't as exciting as an Agent escorting a prisoner, and we don't want to give those who might see us something to talk about."

"Why don't you just ditch the disguise?" she asked.

"Because I'll need it when I come back for Aya."

"You mean when *we* come back for her," Jackie said.

"When *we* come back," he echoed, but he had already decided that it wouldn't be so. After what had happened today, he simply wasn't willing to put her in danger a second time. Jackie wouldn't like it, but Sividious had made up his mind—he would be coming back for Aya alone.

He deactivated the energy shield and made his way out into the large corridor beyond. As he'd predicted, the concession stands were open and spectators were beginning to arrive. Putting on an air of indifference, he made his way toward Portal T16 in a casual, unhurried manner. The few spectators he passed gave him a wide berth and did their best not to look at him. The vendors did likewise, with only one or two of them casting wary glances at the zobo stick dangling from his hip.

He moved past the entrance to Portal T16 and turned into the narrow enclave where a bank of computers was located. Glancing back to make certain he hadn't been followed, he powered on the computer, then pulled out the handheld and plugged it into the docking port. A little red dial appeared in the corner, slowly changing from red to green as the handheld logged him in.

Movement at the edge of his vision caught his attention, and he turned to find Jackie moving into the shadows to join him.

"So what are you doing now?" she asked, scrutinizing the computer screen.

"Logging into the stadium's central computer," he answered. "I'm going to erase the trail left by the AAP." He glanced meaningfully at the Access Pass Jackie wore. "I'm afraid we'll have to destroy yours though."

She frowned at him. "Destroy it? Why?"

"Because if you take it with you to Earth, it will leave a trail for the Agents to follow. They think the one I have is already there, so all I need to do is delete everything between now and just prior to when Aya used it to come to Earth. That way when we use it right now, the trail will end in the same place as before, with Aya fleeing to Earth and leaving the AAP there."

"But won't the Kaladan notice the discrepancy in time between her supposed escape and her appearance in the tournament?"

"I'm hoping no one looks that closely at the records," he told her. "They shouldn't. Aya is still their prisoner. They won't grow suspicious about this AAP until after she vanishes for good. By then it will be too late. Your pass, on the other hand, has never been to Earth. It would be a dead giveaway."

Sighing her frustration at losing her new toy, Jackie removed the lanyard and handed it to him. Sividious entered the pass's serial number into the computer, scanned the records until he found what he wanted, then deleted all records for the past week. He handed the lanyard back to Jackie and watched as she tossed it into a nearby incinerator. It vanished in a flash of red.

Sividious motioned Jackie close and raised his own lanyard. "We can share this one," he said, slipping it over her head so she could read the writings on the computer screen. They were almost cheek to cheek as he continued. "Will you read me the serial number on the AAP?" he asked, his eyes on the computer terminal. "It's on the back."

"K345-876-GCP," she said, and he punched it into the system.

"There's the list of all the shields we deactivated and the security checkpoints we passed through, along with the ID of the computer I accessed in the command center and the railcar we rode in. And the list is much longer than the places we visited today; it goes back for months. This section right here shows the activities of the Agent who had the AAP before Aya stole it from him." He scrolled to the bottom of the page. "And there is the magic little button that will let me scrub the list."

"Don't you need a password or something?"

"The handheld is the password," he told her. "Since only Agents have them, the central computer doesn't question any use of it."

"Sounds to me like they are a bit cocky about their ability to keep a handle on things," Jackie muttered as she ducked out of the lanyard. "But I'm not complaining. Hurry up and nuke that list so we can get out of here."

"Already done," he told her.

She grinned at him. "Must be nice to be such a computer geek," she said playfully.

"My computer skills helped," he told her. "But what I did just now is one of the fundamentals of the Boy Scouts of America."

"And that is . . . ?"

He pulled the handheld from the computer and powered them both off. "To leave no trace," he answered then took her by the hand. "Come on, it's time to go home."

23
PARTNERS IN CRIME

As the brilliant flash of the portal faded behind him, Sividious stared into the darkness of the mine and waited for his eyes to adjust. He was aware that he still held Jackie's hand, but he was unwilling to let go until he could see well enough to not trip over her. That she didn't seem to want to let go either made him smile. It also sent a rush of twitterpated heat through his chest just like it had on the bus earlier in the day.

Was that really only this morning? he wondered. It felt like it had happened days ago.

When his eyes finally adjusted to the dimness, he released Jackie's hand and knelt next to the duffle bag they'd left in the mine. He picked up the stopwatch.

"It shows two hours and twenty minutes," he told her. "That means it's almost six o'clock Earth time."

"It feels more like midnight," Jackie said.

"For you it almost is," he told her. "You were in the stadium for almost seven hours."

"And I nearly got pulverized by Agents," she added then smiled. "But not so much so that I can't come back tomorrow."

"About that," Sividious said. "I was thinking we should wait a couple of days before venturing back in. You know, let things calm down a bit."

She stepped near and looked him right in the eyes. "I know what you're thinking," she said. "And if you go back in without me, I will take you down so hard you will wish you had never been born. And then I will never speak to you again."

He opened his mouth, but she cut him off before he could say anything. "Save it, Sividious," she said. "I've known you too long not to recognize when you are planning something. You gave it away back in the railcar terminal when you said *I* instead of *we*. But I saw it in your eyes even before then. You are afraid for me and don't want to put me in danger, and I appreciate that. It's sweet and chivalrous, and it makes me want to kiss you. But it's also stupid. You need me."

He tried to speak, but once again she cut him off. "Three times I saved your life in there," she insisted. "First with the Agent at the elevator and then again with the werewolf-guard and the freaky robot thing. Without me you would have been captured or killed."

Tears formed in her eyes as she continued. "You would have disappeared, and I would have had no idea what had happened to you. You, Siv. My best friend in the whole world. I don't think I could deal with that." She wiped the tears from her cheeks and forced a laugh. "So don't think for a second that I was any less worried about your safety than you were for mine. I love you, Siv, and we're in this together."

He took her in his arms and hugged her. "All right," he whispered. "I'm sorry. We're in this together."

"And . . . ?" she prompted.

"And so I won't even think about going in without you."

"Dang right you won't," she said, stepping back to look at him. "We're partners in crime." Smiling, she kissed him on the cheek, then bent to retrieve the duffle bag.

Sividious reached up and touched the cheek she had kissed. And he thought he had been twitterpated before! Now he was really fluttery inside. Even worse, he had no idea what he was supposed to do about any of it.

She caught him staring at her, and an amused smile spread across her face. "Don't go all weird on me just because I kissed you on the cheek," she told him. "I'm still your best friend, even if you have finally noticed that I'm a girl." She shooed him away. "So would you mind stepping outside while I change back into my regular clothes?"

He grabbed his things and started down the mine shaft toward the square of light marking the entrance. "I'll change outside," he told her. "I'll wait for you there."

Outside, he hung his backpack on the side of the rusty mine car, then quickly changed back into his school clothes. He was pulling on his shoes when Jackie exited the mine. She carried the duffle bag in one hand and the laser pistol and zobo stick in the other.

"I was wondering," she said, glancing at the weapon. "Do these things work in our world?"

"Yes," he answered. "At least the zobo stick does. I watched the Agents use theirs to shoot Aya. I don't see why the guns wouldn't work as well." He picked up his backpack and slung it over his shoulder. "But since this kind of technology doesn't exist in our world yet, it might be best if others didn't see either weapon. It would draw the wrong kind of attention. I already put mine in my backpack."

Jackie tucked the weapons into her duffle bag, then she and Sividious made their way to the trail that led to the wilderness park. "Can you imagine trying to explain either weapon to your mom?" Jackie said as they started down into the oak brush.

"Can you imagine trying to explain it to the police or the FBI?" Sividious asked. "We would either have to tell them about the stadium or spend the rest of our lives denying accusations that we had ties to some elite, ultra-high-tech terrorist organization."

"I already have some explaining to do." Jackie sighed. "I'm going to have to tell my dad that I lost two of our cattle prods. Either that or I'll need to buy two new ones before he notices they're missing."

"How much are they?"

"About a hundred bucks each," she answered.

Sividious cringed. "Ouch."

"Tell me about it," she said. "And I'll have to buy the stupid things online. There aren't any stores around here that sell them. Even if there were, I doubt a minor can just walk in and purchase one."

"I'll pay for them," Sividious told her. "It's my fault they're gone."

"You're not paying for anything," she countered. "It was my idea to bring them."

"Sorry," he said. "We're partners in crime. That means we share the cost as well as the danger and excitement."

"Fine," she said, her eyes narrowing the way they did right before she hit something. "But you will only pay for one of them." She shook her head. "Man, did you see how that battery pack exploded when the Agent hit your prod with his zobo stick? You're lucky it didn't blow your arm off."

Sividious stopped dead in his tracks. "Uh, where exactly are the cattle prods?" he asked.

"I tossed the one the Agent ruined down an incinerator chute," she said. "I don't know where the other one is. I guess the Agents who captured me have it." Her face grew worried. "That's a problem, isn't it?"

"It might be," he answered. "If the Agents are familiar with our world's technology, they will know the prod came from Portal T16." When Jackie's worried expression deepened, Sividious made a soothing gesture with his hand. "But don't worry about it too much," he told her. "I kind of got the feeling that they don't visit our world very much. We're too primitive technologically to be of much value to them, and we don't have much, if any, magic."

Even as he said it, he realized the flaw in his thinking.

"Then again," he said, rubbing his eyes wearily, "it might very well be *because* Earth's technology is so primitive compared to the stadium's that the Agents will know where to look. They will certainly have categorized each world based on the sophistication of its technology. Considering how many of the stadium's so-called Games revolve around combat, I'm willing to bet the Kaladan have also categorized each world based on the level of sophistication of its weapons."

Reaching into his backpack, he pulled out the handheld and powered it on. Jackie watched nervously while he scrolled through the menus until he found what he was looking for. "Do you want the good news or the bad news?" he asked.

"Bad news first," she answered.

"The bad news is that, yes, Earth is listed among the technologically inferior worlds."

"And the good news?"

"There are twenty-eight other worlds with the same classification."

Jackie relaxed visibly. "Then there's nothing to worry about."

"I guess not," he said, and they started walking again.

Jackie nodded at the handheld. "You probably ought to hide that as well," she told him. "It might look like a smartphone from a distance, but up close, even a moron could see you have an advanced piece of technology. It might be harder to explain than the zobo stick or the laser gun."

"Yeah." Sividious snorted. "And being interrogated by the FBI would be nothing compared to the hostility the Apple Corporation would unleash once they realized their products stink in comparison to this one."

He powered it off and tucked it back into his pack, then he and Jackie made their way down the rest of the trail in silence.

The lack of conversation was fine with Sividious—he had plenty to think about. Unfortunately, his mind kept bouncing between topics as if it were a rubber ball in a blender. So much had happened today to rock his understanding of the universe that he thought it might be weeks before he could come to terms with all of it. If he ever came to terms with it at all.

It made him wonder what his dad would have thought about all of this, and he wished his dad were still around to talk things over with. He knew instinctively that his dad would have believed him about the stadium. Whether or not he would have ventured inside to investigate it for himself was a mystery never to be answered, but Sividious suspected he would have.

Just like I did, he thought and blew out his cheeks wearily. In two short days he had gone from thinking life on other worlds was the stuff of Spielberg and Lucas movies to knowing that all the science fiction in Hollywood didn't hold a candle to the reality of the stadium.

And then there was Jackie.

In two short days she had gone from being "one of the guys" to being an incredibly attractive girl who made his heart beat in strange ways. He shook his head in bewilderment. *Nothing like a little danger to expose one's true feelings,* he thought.

He cast a sideways glance at Jackie. Only it wasn't having his feelings exposed that was making him nuts inside—it was trying to decide what he should do next. Jackie said she would thrash him if he weirded out on her, and he knew she meant it. Maybe it would be best if he pretended that nothing had changed between them. As far as she was concerned, maybe nothing had. Maybe he was the one being irrational about a little kiss on the cheek.

"So tell me about the world where you left the Agent," Jackie said as they were climbing the fence into the wilderness park. "What was it like?"

"It was dead," Sividious answered. He picked up his backpack and waited for Jackie to finish climbing the fence before he continued. "A terrible war had destroyed everything. All the plant life was wilted and decaying. There were no sounds of animal life anywhere. Even the light and air seemed sick." He shook his head. "It had been done with magic, but it looked as bad as the aftermath of a nuclear war."

"Magic," Jackie said. "I never imagined that such a thing could be real."

"Me either," Sividious told her. "I'm still having a hard time getting my head around it. Science, on the other hand, is explainable and understandable because it follows the laws of physics and mathematics. It is methodical and, even more important, *logical.* Even as advanced as Kaladan technology is, it still makes more sense to me than what Aya and Shoar were hurling at one another. Even if I don't fully understand the power source for a zobo stick or a laser gun, I understand the mechanics of such devices well enough to know how to use one. I wouldn't have the slightest idea how to use magic." He pushed a low-hanging branch aside and allowed Jackie to pass, then released the branch and hurried to catch up.

"Maybe magic follows a set of laws that are similar to the laws of science," she suggested. "Maybe it isn't logical in the way we are used to, but it must make sense to the magic wielder or they wouldn't be able to use it."

"I suppose so," Sividious said. "But I'll take technology and rational, logical thought over paranormal weirdness any day."

"So that's what this is about," Jackie said, fixing him with a knowing stare. "You're freaking out because you felt something during Aya's battle with the Dragon Centipede, and it scares you because you can't explain it with science."

Sividious stubbed his toe on a rock and had to flail his arms to keep from falling on his face. When he regained his balance, he turned to look at her. "Are all girls this good at reading people's minds?" he asked.

She smiled at him. "Only those of us who have a vested interest in the person whose mind we are reading," she answered. "It's like having a built-in AAP." She poked him in the arm with her finger. "Besides, I saw the way you acted during the battle—you looked like you were having a heart attack." Her face softened. "So tell me what you felt," she urged. "Maybe we can make sense of it together."

"That's just it," he moaned. "I don't know how to explain it."

"Try," she said.

Sividious sighed. He could see in Jackie's eyes that she wasn't going to let this go until he gave it a shot. It was either talk about it now or spend the next week getting pestered about it.

"It was like a fiery tingle in my chest," he told her. "A rush of energy that washed through me every time Aya or Shoar got ready to do something. It was even sharper during their attacks." He hesitated, searching for the right words. "But the really weird part was how I could *see* some of what they were doing. Not with my eyes, but somewhere inside of me. I could sense their use of magic like it was a part of me."

"It was the AAP," Jackie said. "It had to be. It translates the languages of the all the different worlds directly into your mind. Why would magic be any different?"

"Because," Sividious replied, "I wasn't wearing the AAP at the time."

He could tell by her shocked look that this was something she hadn't expected to hear. But as they exited the wilderness park and started down the street toward Sividious's house, she shook off her surprise and smiled at him. "Then it had something to do with the stadium itself," she said at last. "Maybe the arena acts like a big AAP. It allowed those of us without a lanyard to understand what was being said. It probably made it so you could feel the magic. It's probably part of the show."

"Maybe," he answered, but he was starting to have serious doubts.

She must have heard the uncertainty in his voice because she reached over and took his hand. "Well, whatever the reason, we are in this together." She gave his hand a squeeze. "And look on the bright side," she added. "After we rescue Aya and her cousin, we won't ever have to go back. We can forget the whole thing ever happened."

That last part will be easier said than done, Sividious thought, but he wasn't going to say so to Jackie.

24
NO REST FOR THE WEARY

SIVIDIOUS AND JACKIE WERE COMING up the front walk to his home when the door opened and Simone came out to meet them.

"Where have you two been?" she asked in her best I'm-trying-to-act-like-your-mother voice. "You missed dinner."

"We got hung up at the library," Jackie answered politely. She didn't like Simone very much, but Jackie always did a good job of keeping her feelings hidden. It was one more thing Sividious admired about her. Especially since Simone's tone of voice made him want to smack her. But he always had to remind himself to give her a break. As much as he missed their father, Simone must miss him too, and he figured it was probably harder for a ten-year-old to understand that kind of loss. Still . . .

Simone looked at Jackie's duffle bag. "What's in the bag?"

"My gym clothes," Jackie answered.

Simone's eyes narrowed suspiciously. "It's only Wednesday," she said. "Why are you taking them home?"

"Because she got blood on them when she killed a nosey little brat who wouldn't mind her own business," Sividious growled, losing the battle for civility. "Any more stupid questions?"

"Humph," Simone snorted, huffing herself up as if offended and turning back into the house.

When she was gone, Sividious turned to Jackie. "Sorry about that," he said. "She can really be a snot-face sometimes."

Jackie shrugged. "I'm over it."

"Do you want to take my bike again?" Sividious asked.

"Well, I certainly don't want to walk home," she told him then smiled at Sam as he came out of the house. "Hi, Sam," she said.

"Hey, Jackie," Sam replied. "Hey, I heard what you said about riding Sividious's bike home, but I'm headed out to Kaylee Silmore's house. I can drive you home if you want."

"That would be great," she said. "I am kinda tired."

"You look tired," Sam said. "I'll go start the car." He stopped and looked at Sividious. "Mom's ticked at you for missing dinner," he said. "You might want to tread softly when you go inside."

"Thanks for the warning," Sividious said then turned to Jackie. "I'll see you tomorrow."

"Bye, Siv," she said then followed Sam to the car.

When she was gone, Sividious took a deep breath and went inside to face his mother's wrath.

* * *

Sividious closed his bedroom door behind him and flopped down on his bed. He was exhausted from the events of the past two days, and he had a headache from doing his homework. At least his mother had gone easy on him for missing dinner. After threatening to ground him if it happened again, she had warmed up his dinner and poured him a glass of milk. She had even shooed Simone away when she'd tried to tease him about spending so much time with Jackie.

He looked at the clock and was surprised to find that it was only eight thirty. It felt a lot later than that, and he rubbed his eyes wearily.

Pushing himself into a sitting position, he grabbed his backpack from the corner of his bed and pulled out the handheld. He knew he should go to bed, but he couldn't suppress his curiosity about what other information the tiny computer might contain. He knew he couldn't use it at school. Even Kael, simpleton that he was, would notice how advanced it was. That left only this evening.

He would play with it until ten thirty. Two hours should be more than enough time to familiarize himself with all that it contained. But where to start? Descriptions of worlds? Schedules of events? Profiles of competitors? He shook his head.

No. If he hoped to rescue Aya and her cousin tomorrow, he needed to start with the fundamentals of the stadium itself—its layout, transportation systems, the kinds of beings and robots it employed, security systems, etc. He would need to lay out an escape route that would allow him to see the Kelsprites safely to their world while allowing him to return safely to his own.

Menu after menu, page after page, he scrolled through the information, as excited as a child on an Easter egg hunt as one bit of information led to another even more interesting than the last. Before he knew it, his mother was knocking on his door and telling him to go to bed. When he looked at the clock, he was stunned to find it was eleven fifteen.

"Sorry, Mom," he called. "I was reading and lost track of the time."

"Well, it's lights out," she told him. "You need your rest." Her footsteps moved away down the hall.

Yes, I do, he thought as he turned off his bedroom light, *but I'll rest only* after *I get Aya and her cousin home.*

Pulling the sheet up over his head to hide the glow of the handheld, he continued to learn all he could about the stadium between worlds.

* * *

The next morning, the sound of his alarm clock jolted Sividious awake, and he hurriedly rose and dressed. Even though he'd only gotten a few hours of sleep after finally turning off the handheld, he was excited about what he had learned, and he was eager to share the information with Jackie.

After a quick breakfast, he grabbed what he would need for school then went out to the bus stop to wait.

Brayden Peterson was already there. So were the Hollister twins.

"Did Jackie spend the night again?" Brayden muttered sarcastically.

"You don't see her, do you?" Sividious replied calmly. He wasn't in the mood to deal with Brayden's jealousy and knew the best way to avoid an incident would be to downplay the whole thing.

Brayden scowled at him but didn't say anything more.

A few minutes later, the bus arrived, and Sividious climbed aboard and moved down the aisle to take a seat next to Jackie. Brayden, still scowling, moved clear to the back of the bus.

"You've got that look in your eye," Jackie told him as the bus started down the street.

"What look?"

"The one that says you know something I don't. It's similar to the look you have on test days or right before you give a presentation in science class."

He grinned at her. "I didn't know there was a look for that."

"Well, there is," she told him. "It's smug and arrogant, and it makes most of the kids in class want to punch you in the face, myself included."

"As a matter of fact, I do know something," he told her then cast a look about the bus meaningfully. When he continued, he let his voice drop to a whisper. "But I don't want to talk about it here. There are too many ears."

She narrowed her eyes at him in the way that showed she was irritated with him, and for a moment he thought she might insist. "During lunch, then," she said finally. "If you make me wait until after school, I'll smack you."

He nodded. "During lunch. I'll meet you under the big willow tree by the tennis courts."

* * *

Standing in the shade of the big willow tree, Jackie watched the doors of the school for some sign of Sividious. Dozens of kids had already exited the building and were heading to their favorite spots to eat or to be with friends. Most carried sack lunches, but she spotted a few disposable trays in the hands of those who had already made it through the lunch lines. Out on the lawn beyond the tennis courts, a group of boys was splitting into teams to play football. Kael Jensen was among them.

She glanced back toward the school and found Sividious approaching with a tray of food.

"Sorry it took so long," he apologized. "The lunchroom is a joke. The stupid ninth graders think they can just cut in line." He sat down under the willow and leaned back against the trunk.

"You look tired," she told him as she joined him against the tree. She pulled her sack lunch from her backpack and unwrapped a peanut butter and jelly sandwich.

"I feel tired," he admitted. "But I guess two hours of sleep will do that to a person."

"Then are you sure we should go back in?" she asked.

He nodded. "If we want to do this while Loshar is off duty, it has to be today."

"Okay," she muttered. "But remember that not getting him in trouble is your idea, not mine." She took a bite of her sandwich, then continued speaking around a mouthful of peanut butter. "Why don't we wait until the end of his next shift? It would give you time to rest."

"Because we'd have to miss school on Friday. He isn't off duty during a time that will work for us until Saturday afternoon."

"Saturday is a perfect time to go back in," she insisted then frowned when Sividious shook his head.

"Saturday is the final round of the Jomon tournament," he said darkly. "If we don't have her out of the stadium by then, she will have to fight her cousin."

"Assuming Sheylie wins her semifinal," Jackie said.

"She'll win," Sividious declared. "The Rock Troll she is supposed to face is a weakling. I read his profile on the handheld. The Kaladan have set the whole thing up so that Aya will have to face her cousin."

Jackie was quiet for a moment while she thought about what Sividious had just said. "So what's the plan?"

"We go in today after school," he answered. "I've discovered a route that will get us to both cellblocks with only a minimal risk of running into other beings. It also makes it so we won't have to use the AAP as much, so we will leave less of a trail for Agents to discover."

"And if we do run into other beings?"

"I learned how to set our laser guns to stun," he answered. "So feel free to shoot anything that moves."

Jackie grinned. "With pleasure."

"After we have Aya and Sheylie," Sividious continued, "we will exit Portal G5. It is a world very much like ours, with an almost identical rate of time. Once there, we can use the hyperlink portal I learned about to send Aya and Sheylie home to their world. Then we will use it to return to ours."

"A what kind of portal?"

The smug look Sividious had worn on the bus earlier that day returned, and Jackie knew she'd gotten to the heart of his new knowledge.

"The stadium is pretty much a crossroads for all the different worlds," Sividious explained. "But the passes given to the spectators by the Kaladan grant access only to the portals or gates of the spectators' respective homeworlds. Only the Agents have access to all the worlds. But it wouldn't make sense if each time they wanted to travel to a different world they had to return to the stadium, would it? So the Kaladan created hyperlinks the Agents can use to move directly from one world to another without wasting time returning to the stadium. And the handheld," he added, "is the key to opening the hyperlinks."

"Then why don't we just take Aya and Sheylie to their world and use a hyperlink to come home from there?"

"Because time in our world moves roughly two and a half times faster than it does on Aya's world," he answered. "If something happened and we were delayed for more than ten or twelve hours of her time, more than a day would pass here. Our families would probably call the cops to report us missing."

"What else did you learn last night?" she asked, totally intrigued by this new information.

"A lot," he told her. "Too much to tell you about right now. What do you want to know?"

"I don't know," she said. "Just pick something."

He thought for a moment. "Well, there are three classifications of worlds. Type One worlds are scientific, with technologies ranging from the very primitive to totally awesome *Star Wars*–like things. But they have no magic of any kind. Type Two worlds are both scientific and magical, but the balance between magic and science varies greatly from world to world. Some are more technological, while others are more magical. They are the most common kind of world and make up about 80 percent of all the worlds linked to the stadium. Type Three worlds have only magic. Technology is nonexistent. In fact, the rules governing Type Three worlds make it so that technologies brought in from other worlds won't even function."

"I'll bet that makes the Agents happy," Jackie commented. "So, what is Earth?"

"Earth is a Type Two world, but the balance is more toward science and technology than magic."

"So there is some magic here?"

Sividious nodded. "Yeah, but it's really weak. Aya even said so the first time I met her."

Jackie was quiet as she sorted through the new information. "If the laws of Type Three worlds don't allow for technology, how did the Kaladan link them to the stadium?"

"The stadium itself has a Type Two classification," he answered. "Well, parts of it anyway, such as the arena. That's why Aya was able to use her magic there. And the portals that link the stadium to Type Three worlds were constructed exclusively with magic. They can only be opened by beings with magical abilities. The All Access Passes won't work with them."

"So they aren't really *all* access, then, are they?"

"No. But they do enough. Besides, the Kaladan and their Agents don't really care much for Type Three worlds."

"Unless they need victims for their Games," Jackie said darkly.

"Right."

"So, how do they access the worlds that are exclusively magic?"

"A race of beings called Krogen act as Agents for those worlds. And, after reading their profile, I must say they scare me worse than the regular Agents."

Jackie rubbed her eyes wearily. "Great."

"But look on the bright side. The hyperlinks make it possible to visit other worlds whose rate of time is similar to ours without having to go through the stadium. And the hyperlinks can't access Type Three worlds because the links were created with science instead of magic. But the best part is that the use of hyperlinks isn't logged by the stadium's central computer, so there isn't any way for the Kaladan to trace it back to us."

Jackie took a moment to think about what she'd just heard, then nodded her understanding. "So there's a hyperlink portal here on Earth?"

"Several, actually," Sividious answered. "They are scattered all over the world in most of the major countries. They allow the Agents to cover a lot of ground when they are scouting for recruits for the Games."

"So we could use them to visit places like Germany or Japan?"

Sividious grinned at her. "Cool, huh?"

"Very cool," she answered. "Very cool, indeed."

25
SPECIAL DELIVERY

AFTER SCHOOL, SIVIDIOUS AND JACKIE rode the bus to Sividious's house to get what they needed for their trip into the stadium, then they headed to the abandoned mine and the portal. They were picking their way across the tailings toward the rusted mine car and its stretch of tracks when Sividious pointed to a section of the cliff face to the left of the mine's entrance.

"See that smooth part there near the dead tree?" he asked, and Jackie nodded. "That's the hyperlink portal. It isn't visible unless I activate it with the handheld. The gate that opens into the stadium's sublevels is a short distance down that access road there. Since the gate is used to transport cargo and creatures larger than human-sized life-forms, it requires a larger area than what the mine shaft allows. But like the portal in the mine shaft, it works automatically if you pass through it with a valid AAP.

Jackie did little to hide her surprise. "You mean if you were wearing an Access Pass you could accidentally walk through a portal and find yourself in the lower levels of the stadium?"

"Yeah, but those who have an AAP are supposed to know where the gates are, so it wouldn't be an accident." He fingered the lanyard hanging around his neck for emphasis.

They reached the entrance to the mine, and Jackie set her duffle bag on the ground and unzipped it. When she started to pull out her karate uniform, Sividious stopped her.

"Not this time," he said, pulling a pair of brown hooded robes from his backpack. He handed one to Jackie.

"What is this?" she asked, raising an eyebrow.

"Our disguise for this trip."

"So what are we supposed to be, monks?"

Sividious grinned. "Nope. These are Jedi robes. Sam and I wore them last year for Halloween."

Jackie looked skeptical as she held the robe up to check the fit.

"The hoods will hide our faces from any security cameras that will be running due to the event," he told her. "And we won't have to change out of our regular clothes. These just go on over the top." He put his on and pulled it closed around him. Peering out from under the hood, he added, "But the best part is that these robes look like those worn by the Meesor from a world called Persuolo. They are a religious cult known for their ability to project their thoughts into the minds of other beings. They are even more feared than the Chal'masa because they can use the images they project to cause madness or even to kill."

"So they're homicidal monks," Jackie muttered.

"They can be," Sividious answered. "So it should keep people from wanting to get too close to us." He handed her a strip of white cloth. "Tie this around your waist," he instructed. "It completes the disguise. White shows that we are here as spectators or Owners of some unfortunate recruit. If we wear red, we would give the impression that we have come to compete or that we are hunting someone who wronged us."

"Did you learn all this from the handheld?" she asked.

"Yep. And I've only scratched the surface of the information this little computer contains. It's like having an entire galaxy of information at my fingertips."

Jackie finished tying the white sash around her waist, pulled the hood up over her head, and picked up her duffle bag. She tucked the zobo stick and laser gun inside the folds of her robe then extended her arm to Sividious.

"Shall we?"

Sividious grabbed his backpack before taking her by the arm. "I think we shall," he answered.

They entered the mine and walked slowly as they waited for their eyes to adjust to the darkness. The air grew cool, and the smell of earth filled Sividious's nose. Just short of where the portal stood, dark and invisible to his eyes, he set down his backpack and took Jackie by the hand.

"Almost there," he told her, and she dropped her duffle bag next to his pack.

"Let's do this," she said, and they stepped through in a brilliant flash of white to find themselves in the dimly lit corridor of Portal T16.

At the far end of the corridor, shapes were visible moving in each direction as spectators made their way to the concourses and concession stands. Sividious nodded his satisfaction. He and Jackie should be able to slip into the stream of bodies without too many people realizing where they were coming from.

"The security cameras will be rolling," Sividious told Jackie, "but so long as nothing happens to draw attention to the area, the footage will be autodeleted in four hours. When we reach the main corridor, turn left. We are going to a pneumatic docking bay. It's in a small side corridor just past Portal O16. Unlike the one we used last time, this one isn't used for transportation. The merchants in the sublevels use it to send merchandise up to the vendors of the concession stands. The vendors use it to send payments and invoices and the like. It's also used as a sort of postal system."

"Is it safe for people?"

"Should be," Sividious replied. "The merchants send all kinds of breakable things through it. Eggs. Glass bottles. Live animals and insects."

"Tell me the animals and insects aren't sold as food at the concession stands," she said, a look of horror washing over her face.

"Actually, they are," Sividious told her, "but not a single one of them is cute or cuddly. It's kind of like buying a live lobster at a fancy restaurant."

"That's barbaric," Jackie muttered.

"Welcome to the stadium," Sividious snorted. "Everything about this place is barbaric."

They moved out into the crowd, and it didn't take long for a bubble to form around them as the various beings noticed their attire and gave them a wide berth.

"So much for not drawing the attention of the cameras," Jackie muttered.

"I wouldn't worry about it too much," Sividious whispered. "This is totally normal behavior. The Meesor are frequent visitors. I would be worried if people weren't keeping their distance, because that *would* draw attention to us."

When they reached the pneumatic docking station, they found it already in use by a reptilian creature wearing an apron and what could only be some kind of bizarre chef's hat. Standing in front of a worktable, the creature had its back to them and didn't see them approaching. It simply continued to box up the meal it had prepared then loaded the various containers into a spherical receptacle roughly the size of a trash can. The inside of the sphere contained no shelves or compartments, but each item the chef placed inside it remained precisely where it was, held in place by the antimotion force fields Sividious had read about. The fields were strong enough to keep things from bouncing around, but not so strong as to restrict movement of sentient creatures. Otherwise he and Jackie wouldn't be able to use them.

The lizard chef closed the front of the receptacle, carried it to the far end of the room, then placed it in the pneumatic receiving bay. After punching in the coordinates for delivery, he stepped back.

A moment later the sphere vanished into the wall with a loud *ssshhoomp* of air.

Only then did the creature notice that he and Jackie were watching. Its slitted eyes went wide with fear, and it hurriedly dipped its head.

"Deepest apologies, revered ones," the creature said, its reptilian voice a gravelly hiss. "I did not mean to make you wait."

When the creature remained where it was, Sividious realized it was waiting to be dismissed. He made a soothing gesture with his hand. "Apology accepted," he said softly. "You are free to go."

The creature relaxed visibly, but it kept its head down as it moved past them and out into the main corridor. It vanished into the crowd without looking back.

Sividious led Jackie to the computer terminal near the docking bay. "Anyone can use these," he told her as he punched in the code to order an empty delivery sphere. "You just have to know the codes."

A soft rushing of air sounded, and a sphere dropped into the receiving bay with a gentle *plomp*.

"Climb in," he told her. "I'm sending you to a port on Sublevel 12. I'll be right behind you."

"Are you sure about this?" Jackie asked, the fear in her voice evident. "I'm kind of claustrophobic."

"You'll be there in less than ten seconds," he soothed. "Just close your eyes and pretend you're on a ride at Disneyland."

"Yeah, right," she grumbled, but she climbed in anyway. When she was ready, she gave him a thumbs-up and closed the front of the sphere.

He pressed the button that sent her rushing toward Sublevel 12 then ordered an empty sphere for himself.

Now came the tricky part.

The system wasn't meant to be used as a mode of transportation, so there wasn't any way to launch a delivery from inside a sphere—it had to be done from the external computer terminal. The good news was that a sphere wouldn't launch if its door was ajar, so all he had to do was leave the door open while he punched in the destination code. Then he could climb in, situate himself, and shut the door. The system would then launch him automatically. The problem was that he only had five seconds from the time he punched in the code until he had to shut the door. If he wasn't fast enough, the launch would abort.

It took him four tries.

On the fourth attempt, he didn't worry about situating himself comfortably and just dove in. He vanished into darkness with a loud *ssshhoomp.* Ten seconds later he was climbing out of the sphere to face an angry Jackie.

"What took you so long?" she demanded. "I was starting to think you weren't coming."

"When you're the cargo, it's a little harder to launch one of these on your own," he told her then stiffened in surprise when he noticed two bodies lying on the floor behind her. At first they looked like they were wearing body armor, but he quickly realized the armor was really the exoskeleton of two giant insects. They looked a great deal like praying mantises. "Uh, who are they?"

"I don't know," Jackie replied. "I didn't wait to find out before I shot them."

"Stunned, I hope?"

She frowned at him. "I'm not a murderer. Of course I used stun." She shrugged. "Besides, I didn't have time to switch it back to its lethal setting. The things came after me the moment I climbed out of the sphere."

"They must have realized you weren't a real Meesor," Sividious said then flinched as Jackie raised an eyebrow at him.

"Ya think?" she muttered sarcastically. "I wonder what could have given them that idea." She kicked the empty sphere for emphasis. She looked at the bug things. "So what do we do with them?"

"Leave them," Sividious said. "They'll be out for a while."

Jackie nudged one with her foot. "Too bad the bug collection project for biology was due last week," she muttered. "This one would have made a fine specimen."

"Right up until Miss Johnson died of a heart attack," Sividious told her then looked at the bug. "What would you pin it with, rebar?"

Jackie slapped him in the arm. "Don't be gross."

"You started it," he told her then pulled his hood up over his face and moved to the end of the room to peer out at the wide expanse that was the corridor of gates. Like the last time he'd seen it, it was a hive of activity, and beings of every shape and size were moving about.

"Which way?" Jackie whispered as she moved up next to him.

"Right," he answered. "The hallway we want will be the fourth one from where we are now." He pointed to a stack of crates near a large antigravity sled. "That's the spot where the Gordorian Firetoads blew up the load of fireworks when we were down here with Loshar. The entrance to the cellblock is just beyond it."

"Lead the way," Jackie said, and together they moved out into the corridor.

26
AVENGING ANGEL

LIKE THE BEINGS IN THE upper levels, those working here made way for Jackie and Sividious to pass, but the size of the bubble around them was considerably smaller than it had been in the upper levels. Even the looks she and Sividious were getting were different. She saw much more curiosity than fear. On a few faces she even saw what could only be described as respect.

It made Jackie wonder if the merchants were too busy in their trading and shipping to care about giving a pair of Meesor a wide berth or if they were so accustomed to danger due to the kinds of creatures they dealt with that they simply weren't afraid. She decided it didn't matter so long as no one tried to stop them.

No one did, and she and Sividious made it to the corridor leading to the Locker Rooms without any trouble. They walked quickly, moving like they had a purpose. A moment later they reached the shimmering energy shield marking the entrance to Aya's cellblock.

It deactivated in response to Sividious's AAP, and Jackie followed him through without slowing. Fifty yards later, Sividious took her by the sleeve and stopped.

"This is Aya's cell," he whispered. "F7-55R. But we can't deactivate the shield without alerting whoever is on duty at the command center."

"So I should probably take him out, don't you think?" She heard the excitement in her voice, but she didn't care. She liked using the laser gun. It made her feel powerful. Even more important, it made her feel like she wasn't just along for the ride but truly contributing something to the mission to free Aya.

Sividious chuckled inside his hood. "Do you think you can stun him without damaging anything or alerting the backup robot guards?" he asked.

"Piece of cake," she replied, pulling her laser gun out of her robe. "He'll never even know what hit him."

"Once he's out," Sividious continued, "you'll need to climb up into the command center and deactivate the shield on Aya's cell." He handed her the AAP, and she put it on. "This will let you read the markings on the control panel. Remember, F7-55R. Once you've killed the shield, come back here. We will go back the way we came."

"Why don't we use the AAP to let her out?" Jackie asked.

"Less of a trail for me to have to erase later," he answered then urged her forward with a nod. "Go on," he said. "We'll wait for you here."

Leaving Sividious to stand in front of the shimmering wall of energy, Jackie hid her hands inside the sleeves of the robe and folded her arms as if meditating. Her finger was light on the trigger even as she tightened her hold on the gun's grip. Moving into the large, octagonal room of the command center, she flipped the weapon's safety off. The guard, a bird-like creature with a razor-sharp beak and large, luminous eyes, was in for a nasty surprise.

The bird-thing saw her enter, took one look at her robe, then lowered its eyes. "May I help you, honorable Meesor?" it asked as Jackie neared the center console. When she didn't answer, the tall feathers on the back of the creature's neck began to twitch nervously, but it still didn't lift its head to look at her. A moment later it slumped against the control panel as she shot it with a single burst of brilliant blue energy.

"No thanks," she muttered as she climbed the ladder into the command center. "I can do this myself."

She pulled the unconscious bird-thing off the console. As it slumped backward in its chair, she pressed the button that would let Aya out of her cell.

Her task complete, she took the guard's Access Pass and jumped down from the command center.

* * *

When the energy shield on Aya's cell vanished, Sividious pulled the hood from his head and stepped inside.

"Aya," he said gently but froze when he saw her curled up in a ball in a corner with her wings spread on the floor behind her. He couldn't see her face, but he could tell from the tremors rocking her body that she was crying.

"Aya," he said again, and this time she turned to look at him. Her beautiful blue face was streaked with tears.

Her eyes went wide when she recognized him, and she leapt to her feet and rushed forward to hug him. Squeezing him tightly, she began chattering in her bizarre, insect-like language.

"I can't understand you," he told her then stepped back and shook his head, tapping his ear for emphasis.

"She said she's glad to see you," Jackie said from behind him, "but that we have come too late."

"Too late for what?" he asked.

"Ask her," Jackie said, handing him two lanyards. One was his AAP. The other . . .

"Where did you get this?"

"From the guard." She tapped a third lanyard hanging around her neck. "I borrowed this one from the guest pass compartment Loshar used."

"Good thinking," Sividious told her as he put on his AAP. He handed the other one to Aya.

"You said we came too late," Sividious said once Aya had the lanyard on. "Too late for what?"

"To get me out," Aya answered. "I cannot leave now."

"Of course you can," he insisted. "And we're taking your cousin out too. I've already worked out how—"

She placed a finger on his lips to silence him.

"Sheylie is dead," Aya said, anguish heavy in her voice. "She was killed during her match with the Rock Troll yesterday."

Sividious felt as if he'd been kicked in the stomach. "Dead? But she was more than a match for the Rock Troll. I read it on this." He showed her the handheld. "She should have defeated him easily."

Tears welled up in Aya's eyes. "She did it for me," she sobbed. "She deliberately lost the match so she would not have to face me in the final round." Her slender frame trembled as a wave of grief washed through her. "She didn't even try to defend herself. She just stood there and let the Rock Troll kill her."

Tears formed in Sividious's eyes as he took Aya in his arms and hugged her. "I'm sorry," he whispered then glanced at Jackie and found that her eyes were wet as well. "This is my fault," he told Aya. "I should have come sooner."

"No," she said quietly. "The blame lies with the Kaladan. They knew that if Sheylie and I faced one another in the final match, we would not fight. And such a refusal is, in the eyes of the Kaladan, the greatest of sins. They would have been able to pronounce forfeiture on both of us and send us to the mines on Kaladan. What they didn't count on was Sheylie's willingness to sacrifice herself to thwart their twisted plan."

She hesitated, choking on her sorrow, then shook herself and continued. "By losing, Sheylie not only spared me the hell of the mines, but she opened the way for me to earn my Free Agent status." She determinedly brushed the tears away. "And I intend to do just that. I will avenge my cousin's death and claim the prize the Kaladan have gone to such extreme lengths to keep me from getting."

"But you don't need it," Jackie insisted. "We can take you home right now. You don't need to win the tournament. You'll never have to set foot in this place again."

"Right," Sividious agreed, but Aya was shaking her head.

"I will avenge my cousin," she said. "I must."

Sividious wanted to argue the matter further, but he could see in Aya's eyes that it would do no good. Her mind was made up.

She reached up and touched his cheek. "I'm sorry to have put you through so much trouble," she told him. "You risked your life for me. I will never forget that. You have become a true and dear friend, and I don't even know your name."

"Sividious Stark," he told her then took her by the hand. "Are you sure you won't reconsider? I can have you back home within the hour."

Aya shook her head. "After I avenge my cousin and win the Jomon tournament," Aya said, "I will be free to return to my homeworld. My Free Agent status will ensure that the Kaladan and their Secret Police won't come looking for me."

She took a step backward and smiled. "Farewell, Sividious Stark," she said. "I will never forget you."

* * *

"Well, that stinks," Jackie muttered as they made their way back to the command center to reactivate the shield on Aya's cell and return the borrowed Access Passes.

"Tell me about it," Sividious mumbled. He had never been so disappointed in his life. After all he and Jackie had done—after all they had risked—he couldn't believe that Aya had refused to come with them. Her love for her cousin must be strong for her to want to risk another battle. Especially since there was no telling what the Kaladan might do now that Aya was on the verge of winning Free Agent status.

The thought stopped him dead in his tracks.

"What is it?" Jackie asked, raising her laser gun and casting about for enemies.

"I was just thinking about the Kaladan notion of fairness," Sividious told her. "And I'm pretty sure that Aya won't have as easy a time winning her Free Agent status as she might think."

"So what do we do about it?" Jackie asked. "Haul her out of here by force?"

"As much as I'd like to," Sividious said, "I don't think we could pull it off without getting caught ourselves."

"So what is your plan?" she asked. "I can see by the look in your eyes that you have one."

"We come back on Saturday to watch her match against the Rock Troll," Sividious answered. "I'll figure out the rest between now and then."

Jackie sighed her displeasure. "Just when I was starting to think we would never have to come back to this stupid place . . ."

"I know," he said. "But I don't see what else we can do. Maybe after Aya wins the match—and I'm certain she will—the Kaladan will allow her to leave. Maybe they won't have any choice."

"And maybe pigs will learn how to fly," Jackie muttered.

Sividious stared at her without amusement. "Considering where we are, I don't think flying pigs are out of the question."

"Then neither is a Kaladan double cross," she told him.

Sividious nodded. "I know. That's why I am going to learn everything I can about Free Agent status. Come on, let's get out of here."

They returned to Portal T16 the same way they came in, using the pneumatic delivery tubes to bypass all but one of the security checkpoints. Once there, Sividious used the handheld to log into the stadium's central computer and delete all references to his stolen AAP. With that complete, he updated the information in the handheld by synchronizing it with the central computer's newest time stamp of information. He hoped this newest information would give him some insight into what the Kaladan were planning. If not . . .

He tried not to think about what *if not* might mean.

Pulling the handheld from its docking port, he joined Jackie where she waited for him in front of the shimmering wall of the portal. He took her by the hand, and they passed through to Earth in a flash of white.

27
AN ALTERNATE ROUTE

When Saturday afternoon finally arrived, Sividious felt like he'd been waiting for two months instead of just two days. He was nervous and antsy, and he hadn't slept for longer than three hours either night. He'd tried busying himself with chores and homework, but even putting the finishing touches on his science project hadn't helped to pass the time any quicker.

And yet part of him wished Aya's match wasn't for another week.

"You don't look so good," Jackie said when she arrived at his house on her bike. She dropped it on the lawn and joined him on the front porch. "You aren't sick, are you?"

"Just worried," he said. "I've read everything there is on the roles and rights of Free Agents, and I didn't find anything to indicate that the Kaladan can withhold the honor from Aya once she wins the Jomon tournament. She will be free to return to her homeworld, and she will never have to compete again unless she chooses to."

"Why would she choose to?" Jackie asked.

"Every so often, the Tournament of Champions is held," Sividious told her. "It's for Free Agents who have won any of the tournaments the stadium holds. The winner of this tournament is granted a special kind of Free Agent status called Intergalactic Immunity. They are given an AAP like those the Agents have, and they are free to visit any world they choose. They are also granted Owner privileges and given a substantial amount of money with which they can purchase competitors of their own. In essence, they become slave owners like the Kaladan and the other scumbag Owners we saw in the lounges in the sublevels."

"But Aya would never do any of that," Jackie insisted.

"I know. That's why the Kaladan have tried so hard to keep her from winning. They don't want to waste their precious awards on someone who will refuse to use them."

"But if she doesn't use them, the Kaladan aren't out anything. Why are they worried about it?"

"I don't know. But if I had to guess, I'd say it's a pride thing. The Kaladan don't like the idea of someone bucking their precious system. Aya already showed she's willing to ignore their rules when she didn't kill the Dragon Centipede. I looked up her record and found that she did the same thing with every other competitor she faced. She didn't kill any of them. The crowd loves how merciful she is, but the Kaladan hate it. The very notion of sparing your competitor is offensive to them. In their eyes, it undermines the validity of the Games and sets a bad precedent. If every competitor were to be as merciful as Aya, the Kaladan would lose their enterprise."

"So they've been trying to set her up to lose," Jackie said. "Kill or be killed, is that it?"

Sividious nodded. "Looks that way. If she is killed, the Kaladan win because they don't have to give her anything. If she kills, the Kaladan still win because she played according to their rules and validated their games."

Jackie's eyes were troubled as she thought about that. Finally she said, "She's going to kill the Rock Troll, isn't she, to avenge her cousin's death."

"Looks that way."

"And then the Kaladan will still find some way to keep from awarding her Free Agent status."

"Probably."

"So, do you have a plan for getting her out after the Kaladan prove us right about their notion of fairness?"

Sividious nodded. "Yep. But this time we'll meet her in the tunnel as she exits the field. We'll escort her to Portal C2—another world with a rate of time very similar to Earth's—and then use a hyperlink to get her and us home."

"Sounds too easy," Jackie said. "What's the catch?"

"We'll have to take out six or more Agents to do it."

Jackie stared at him as if he'd lost his mind. "And how are we going to do that?"

"With the laser guns, of course, but we'll need to do it quickly, before anyone realizes what's happening. I don't want to get into a firefight with Agents, because they won't be using stun."

"Then neither will I," Jackie said.

Sividious shook his head. "Stunning them will be bad enough. If we kill any of them, we might find ourselves at the top of the Kaladan's most-wanted list instead of just somewhere in the middle of it."

"They have a most-wanted list?" she asked. "Like, 'Hey, America, if you've seen this guy, help us bring him to justice' most-wanted list?"

"Yep. Only the Kaladan use Agents and bounty hunters to track criminals down—dead or alive."

"Stun it is, then," she said then mumbled something else that Sividious couldn't quite make out, but he was pretty sure he heard the words *zobo stick*.

He handed her a duffle bag.

"What's this?"

"Our disguise for today," he told her. "It's something a little less conspicuous than the Chal'masa and Meesor outfits."

Jackie unzipped the bag and peered inside. "Where did you get these?"

"From the wardrobe in the drama room at school," he answered with a smile. "I sneaked them out during lunch yesterday. They won't be missed. The drama class is doing *Guys and Dolls* right now."

"And these are for . . . ?"

"Something Shakespeare, I think," he said. "The old English peasant look is surprisingly common on many of the worlds inhabited by creatures like Aya."

"And you know all this because . . . ?"

"Because I haven't slept in three days," he answered then pulled the handheld out of his pocket far enough for her to see.

She nodded her understanding. "I really ought to get myself one of those," she muttered.

"You really shouldn't," he countered. "They keep you from getting any sleep."

Jackie stood. "So are we going, or what?"

Sividious pushed himself up off the porch. "We're going," he told her, and they started down the walk.

* * *

As Sividious and Jackie rose from the porch, Sam eased the front door the rest of the way closed and stood where he was for a moment, trying to piece together what he had just heard. It hadn't been much, since the two had kept their voices down and he'd had to listen through a narrow crack, but it was enough to concern him.

He didn't normally spy on his little brother. In fact, this was the first time he'd done so in more than five years. But Siv had been acting so weird the past week Sam had started to worry that something might be wrong with him.

There was.

His little brother was delusional. So was Jackie, for that matter. She had to be to have become so immersed in whatever science fiction/fantasy weirdness Siv had dreamed up.

Sam shook his head. Then again, there had to be some kind of logical explanation for this. They couldn't both be crazy, could they? Maybe it was some kind of role-playing game like Dungeons and Dragons.

He frowned. Either way, Siv was way too into the whole thing, especially if he was losing sleep because of it.

He peered out the window to see Sividious and Jackie disappear behind the hedges in front of the Jacobson home at the end of the street. They looked to be heading for the wilderness park. That must be where they played the game.

He momentarily considered following them, then shrugged it off. He supposed there were worse things the two could be doing. It wasn't like they were doing anything illegal or dangerous. He supposed he could let the weirdness of it all slide. It might even be good for Siv—maybe these fantasy worlds he had created were his way of dealing with their father's death.

He hoped so because he didn't want to think Sividious might be losing his mind. If it went on for too much longer, he'd talk to Sividious about it. Until then, he would let his little brother enjoy his fantasy worlds.

* * *

When Jackie and Sividious reached the abandoned mine, they took turns changing into their disguises then stashed their everyday clothes in their duffle bags and hid them among the rubble littering the dimly lit shaft. Jackie started to move deeper into the mine toward the portal, but Sividious called her back.

"We aren't going that way this time," he told her, motioning for her to follow him back outside.

"So which way are we going?" she asked. She knew Sividious probably had a good reason for what he was planning, but she didn't like last-minute surprises. When she told him so, he apologized.

"Sorry," he said, sounding like he meant it. "I've just got so many things running through my mind that I can't remember what I have told you and what I haven't."

"It's okay," she said, shrugging. "I just do better when I know the plan."

"We're going to use the hyperlink to travel to a world called Palinor. It is the one I told you about earlier, the one with a similar rate of time to Earth's. Palinor is connected to the stadium by Portal C2, the one I hope to use to take Aya out of the stadium. That way when the Kaladan trace the AAP, it won't lead to or from Earth. We'll be covering our tracks even as we are making them."

"Why don't you just use the handheld to log into the computer and erase it like you did last time?" she asked.

"I won't have time," he told her. "Things are going to get really crazy once we have Aya. Especially if there are Agents trying to stop us." He smiled. "The good thing is once they realize Aya is trying to escape, they will automatically assume she is trying to do so through the portal leading to her homeworld. They will try to intercept her there. The bad thing is the security cameras will be rolling, so it won't take the Agents long to figure out where we are. They'll come for us on Palinor."

His smile deepened into one of extreme satisfaction. "But since we will be using the hyperlink, they will have no way of tracing us any farther than that. They might even believe it is our homeworld and think we are still there."

"It's a good plan," Jackie told him then added a silent, *assuming we don't get killed in the process.*

They moved to the cliff face Sividious had pointed out on Thursday, and Jackie watched in amazement as Sividious used the handheld to activate the hyperlink. He punched in a series of numbers, and a hint of blue light shot from the end of the tiny computer. The light moved across the smooth stone in a shimmering of tight lines that reminded Jackie of a bar-code scanner at a grocery store. When it had scanned the entire length of the stone, moving from top to bottom, it vanished. A heartbeat later so did the stone. In its place stood a glowing circle of white light, a swirling, pulsating sea of fire that looked as if it would incinerate anything that moved too close.

"We're going through *that?*" she asked incredulously.

"Pretty impressive, huh?" he replied, his eyes alight with the hyperlink's fiery glow.

"Uh . . . it makes me feel like a mosquito staring into a bug zapper," she told him. "Are you sure it's safe?"

"Perfectly," he replied with a smile. "And the cool part is anyone or anything can pass through it. You don't need an AAP."

She stared at the fiery hole a moment longer then took a deep breath and let it out slowly. "What are we going to find on the other side?"

"A forest of giant trees," Sividious answered. "Just think of it as Endor without any Ewoks."

"Will there be *any* creatures or beings in the area?"

"There shouldn't be," Sividious told her. "The Kaladan set all the portal and hyperlink points in secluded or relatively out-of-the-way places like where we are now." He gestured at the abandoned mine road.

Jackie wasn't convinced. She pulled the laser gun from beneath the tunic Sividious had given her and leveled the weapon before her. "Well, I'm not taking any chances," she told him.

Sividious motioned her forward. "Let's go."

Tightening her grip on the gun, Jackie squinted against the brightness and stepped into the light—

And found herself standing amid the roots of the largest trees she had ever seen. The roots alone were as tall as the trees back on Earth and formed a labyrinth of gnarled wood that snaked away into shadow. And the trees . . .

She shook her head in awe. The trees were thousands of feet tall, with trunks as thick as skyscrapers. The sight reminded her of her trip to New York City last year and how small she had felt while staring up at the Empire State Building. Except that in New York she had still been able to see the sky—here, nothing was visible but a dense canopy of green and brown stretching as far as she could see. The air was rich with the smell of loam, and the sounds of birds echoed through the canopy high overhead.

"Impressive, isn't it?" Sividious asked from beside her, and she flinched. She hadn't heard him join her.

"This is what Earth must look like to an ant," she muttered. "And I don't like it. Makes me feel way too small and vulnerable."

"Don't worry," Sividious said. "The only things on this world that are big are the trees." He turned toward the hyperlink still glowing behind him. "And we aren't staying very long, anyway." He pressed a button on the handheld, and the fan of blue light that was the computer's scanner moved over the surface of the hyperlink. The swirl of white fire altered direction slightly then continued to spin and pulsate like before.

"Let's go," Sividious said. "The stadium awaits."

28
STACKING THE ODDS

WHEN SIVIDIOUS AND JACKIE ARRIVED in the stadium through Portal C2, they found a crowd of bird-like beings moving down the corridor ahead of them. Roughly the height of a human, the creatures walked on two legs and had a pair of arms in addition to a set of sleek muscular wings. Their hands and feet sported eagle-like talons, and large luminous eyes and hooked beaks graced each of their feathered heads. Their sleek bodies were covered with gray-black feathers, and they were naked save for a pair of tight-fitting pants made of soft leather. They moved away in a series of harsh chirps and clicks. That Sividious couldn't understand them reminded him that he wasn't wearing the AAP. Pulling it from his pocket, he put it on and tucked it beneath his tunic.

"Those are Riyon," Sividious told Jackie. "One of the flying races of beings from Palinor. There are several types that all live in the canopy of the giant trees you saw there. They have entire cities up in the branches."

He gestured back at the shimmering wall of the portal. "But don't worry. I used the handheld to program the AAP. When we leave the stadium, the portal will deposit us somewhere on the ground near one of the Noysar cities. They are the humanoid ground-dwellers of Palinor." He patted the handheld in his pocket. "I've already located a nearby hyperlink so we can send Aya home."

When Jackie nodded without speaking, Sividious knew she was on edge. He took her by the hand and waited until she looked at him.

"It's going to be okay," he told her. "We'll be out of here in no time." Before he could say anything more, the portal flashed behind them, and he and Jackie turned to find a pair of very human-looking beings coming toward them. They were dressed in the same Shakespearian-type clothes he and Jackie wore.

The pair nodded as they passed, and Sividious returned the greeting in similar fashion. When the two were out of earshot, Sividious continued.

"See?" he said with a smile. "A little research goes a long way. Even those Palinorians didn't realize we aren't from their world. If, or when, the Kaladan Agents look at surveillance video, they won't see anything that will link us to Earth."

They followed the Palinorian humanoids into the main corridor, then merged into a crowd of other humanoids moving toward the concourses. "We'll watch from the entrance," Sividious whispered. "If there are any seats that aren't taken by the time Aya is ready to compete, we'll take them."

"And risk another encounter with werewolf commandos, most likely," Jackie muttered.

"Not this time," Sividious assured her. "I checked. Most of the spectators on this level are politicians or nobles from Type Three worlds. Sure they have magic they could use on us, but I doubt they will. They won't want to cause trouble for fear of losing their viewing privileges. Remember, they only make up about 10 percent of all the worlds present anyway. If they do something to anger the Kaladan, they will find themselves locked out of the stadium for good. Or their worlds might be plundered for whatever creatures the Kaladan can use in the Games."

"Is there anything you haven't thought of?"

"Probably," he admitted. "But we'll cross that bridge if we come to it." He took her by the arm and guided her to the side of a concourse entrance, where they could look down at the bleachers.

Beings and creatures of every kind filed past as he and Jackie waited, and Sividious picked up bits and pieces of a dozen different conversations. Most of them concerned Aya and included predictions about how she would fare against the Rock Troll. It was obvious that the majority of the spectators were rooting for the young Kelsprite and fully expected her to win. The few who were speaking highly of the Rock Troll looked like trolls themselves, grotesque-looking things that were more animal than humanoid. They reminded Sividious of orcs from *The Lord of the Rings*.

He could tell by the way Jackie was eyeing them that she was contemplating shooting them with her laser gun at the first hint of a threat.

A group of young humanoids, who didn't look all that different from kids he and Jackie might go to school with, walked by, and Sividious picked up their conversation.

"It's too bad Polo and Yasela couldn't come," one of the beings said. "They would have loved to see Aya smash the Rock Troll."

"I know," added another. "Polo especially. He is totally obsessed with Aya."

"He's in love with her," said the first. "It's weird. I mean, she's pretty and all, but . . ." The rest of the conversation faded into the noise of the crowd.

Sividious watched them take their seats then leaned close to Jackie. "I know where we can sit," he whispered. "But we'll wait until the stadium translator is activated. If the beings in this area found out I was using an AAP to understand them, they might get mad."

Ten minutes passed before the loud hum Sividious was waiting for filled the stadium. Once again, it was an odd pulsing sound that moved from high to low as if someone were trying to tune a radio to the proper channel. As soon as the hum faded, the hodgepodge of languages being spoken around them became one language.

"Let's go," Sividious said, starting down the stairs.

"Excuse me," he said as he reached the row occupied by the young humanoids. "Are these seats going to be used during the tournament? My friend and I have seats near the top of this section, but we would love to be closer to the action if you would allow it."

"Go right ahead," the nearest female said. "Two of our friends aren't coming."

"Thank you," Sividious said. "If they do end up coming, we will gladly move."

The young female smiled. "I'm Glora," she said by way of introduction. "This is Rommis, and this is Daker." She pointed to the males sitting next to her. "And next to them are Kylila and Veisra." The two young ladies each gave a little wave as they were introduced.

"I'm Albert," he answered, "and this is Marie. Thanks again for letting us sit with you."

"No problem," Glora said.

"So are you here to see Aya or the Rock Troll?" Rommis asked.

"Aya," Siv answered. "She's been my favorite since the moment she entered the Games."

"Ours too," Glora said. "I hope she wins it all."

"So do I," Sividious said then turned to study the playing field, content to let the conversation die. When Glora and her friends resumed talking among themselves, Sividious leaned close to Jackie.

"After Aya wins, she'll probably go out through that tunnel there." He pointed to a dark opening on the right side of the arena. "It's the shortest path to the portal leading to her homeworld. But since we don't know for sure which way she will go, we'll just have to wait and see. Once we know her path, we can move to intercept her. The arena level is restricted to all but those who have an AAP, so she shouldn't be too hard to find."

Jackie's face scrunched angrily. "Especially since she'll likely be surrounded by Kaladan Agents."

Before Sividious could respond, the gigantic video screens towering above the spectators flared to life, and for the next five minutes, commercials from a dozen worlds flashed brightly, encouraging people to visit the concession stands. When the commercials finally ended, the face of the beautiful female announcer appeared. Green eyes sparkling, her purple face split into a toothy smile as she greeted the spectators.

"Welcome, citizens of the universe, to the Jomon Worlds of Magic Tournament. Today's final match features Aya the Kelsprite from the world of Fallisor, and Lazacor the Rock Troll from the world of Doromara."

The stadium erupted in cheers, most of them for Aya, and the announcer smiled as she waited for the noise to subside. "As you know," she said at last, "the winner of today's tournament will receive Free Agent status and all the rights and privileges associated with it."

She fell silent again as the majority of the spectators began chanting, "Aya! Aya! Aya!" and it was several minutes before it quieted enough for her to add, "Prepare the field."

This time the roar of the crowd was deafening, and Sividious put his fingers in his ears to drown out the noise as he turned his attention to the floor of the arena. Today it was brown and looked like loose dirt, and the obstacles emerging from it—an assortment of pillars and walls and blocks—all appeared to be made of rough-hewn sandstone. The floating obstacles moving in from a large side door, however, were jet black in color, and many were covered with spikes or rows of sharpened blades. They settled into place at different heights above the playing field.

The look of the arena was so different from the last time Aya had competed that Sividious immediately suspected the Kaladan of foul play. A moment later his suspicion was confirmed when the Rock Troll made his way out of the tunnel and onto the field.

The creature's skin was the same color as the brownish obstacles on the field and looked like it was made of the same rough sandstone. The troll was stocky and thick limbed and blended in so completely with his surroundings that when he stopped, he nearly disappeared from view. He carried a dull metal shield in one hand and a stout cudgel in the other. His eyes were tiny orbs of unblinking black.

"The Kaladan aren't very subtle about trying to rig this match in favor of the troll, are they?" Jackie muttered angrily.

Two creatures in the row in front of her turned around to glare at her. They were humanoid in shape, but their skin was as rough as tree bark. "The Rock Troll can't fly," they grumbled. "The Kaladan are simply trying to level the playing field."

"So what do you call that?" Sividious asked, pointing to the overhead lights, which had already started to dim. Within moments the upper levels of the stadium were lost in darkness and the night sky was visible in all its starry glory. The floating obstacles had all but vanished into the gloom.

It was a gloom, Sividious realized, that would be even more pronounced from the playing field because of the lights shining from the top of the arena wall. Aya would be blinded to everything but that which was on the ground. Any attempt to fly during the match risked a collision with the floating obstacles.

He leaned toward the two bark-faced creatures. "The Kaladan must think the Rock Troll is a pathetic weakling If they need to go to such lengths to 'level the playing field,' as you call it."

"Lazacor is no weakling," one of the creatures growled, the creases on its bark-like face tightening in anger.

"Then my earlier statement holds true," Jackie told it. "The Kaladan are rigging the match against Aya."

As if to confirm her words, an uneasy chorus of boos rose from the crowd as they too realized the young Kelsprite would be at a marked disadvantage.

A pair of spotlights zeroed in on one of the tunnels as Aya emerged into the bright glare. She shielded her eyes with one hand and glanced around the arena. Even from such a distance, Sividious could tell she was scowling.

Spreading her wings up over her head, she cupped them in a shield against the bright light and made her way to the blue platform rising from the arena. With her slender face lost in shadow, she stood atop the platform and waited for the Rock Troll to take his position as well.

As soon as he was in place, the voice of the announcer echoed through the stadium.

"Let the final match begin."

29
THE JOMON FINAL

STANDING ATOP HER PLATFORM, AYA watched from within the shadow of her wings as the Rock Troll made his way toward his own starting point. Her heart burned with anger as she thought about how mercilessly the troll had killed Sheylie. Her cousin hadn't even tried to defend herself as Lazacor rushed upon her, crushing her with one violent stroke of his cudgel. She could have defeated him easily, could have burned him from existence with a powerful burst of her fiery magic.

Aya narrowed her eyes determinedly. It was the same fiery magic she possessed, a fact the Rock Troll was about to discover. It mattered little that the Kaladan were trying to stack the odds in the troll's favor. It mattered even less that they would gain the victory no matter what the outcome of the match might be. She wasn't doing this for herself, and she wasn't doing it to appease Kaladan vanity. She was doing it for Sheylie.

Focusing her attention on the Rock Troll's beady, emotionless eyes, she reached into that part of herself that was her magic and prepared to burn the vile creature to a cinder.

Suddenly the Rock Troll lurched forward with incredible speed.

Aya met its charge with a swirling jet of white-hot fire, knocking it from its feet and slamming it backward into a stone wall. The wall exploded into fragments that flared to ash as the fire swallowed them, and the entire area around Lazacor vanished in heat and smoke.

She could feel the troll moving beneath the onslaught of fire, but his movements were neither anguished nor rushed. He emerged a moment later completely unscathed, his heavily muscled body wrapped in a shroud of gray-green shadow. She knew instinctively that the impenetrable aura of magic was something Rock Trolls didn't possess naturally. Some other power was at work here, some kind of magic she'd never encountered before. It wasn't emanating *from* the troll but from somewhere *on* the troll. The miserable creature was getting help—he was cheating!

She attacked again, hammering the troll with fire even more intense than before, but it slid off the dark aura protecting him like water sliding off an oiled canvas. The deflected streamers of fiery magic burned holes in nearby walls and ignited a section of the arena floor. Completely unscathed by the attack—an attack which should have seared the creature's flesh from its bones—Lazacor advanced through the maelstrom unharmed.

Aya watched in disbelief as the troll raised his cudgel and sent a burst of red fire lancing toward her with such tremendous speed she barely managed to turn it aside. Even then some of it burned through the protective barrier she pulled around herself, singeing her clothes and hair and scorching part of her left wing.

The pain woke her to the seriousness of the situation, and she did the only thing she could—she launched herself into the air and winged it up into the darkness. She would rather risk the spikes and blades of the floating obstacles than risk doing battle with a magic much more powerful than her own.

Using the backdrop of stars and galaxies to silhouette the obstacles, she flew as quickly as she dared, her mind working furiously on a plan for defeating the troll's mysterious counterpart.

* * *

Sividious watched Aya disappear into the darkness above the playing field, then turned his attention back to the group of young people sitting beside him. They had erupted into anger the moment the Rock Troll used his magic, filling the air with curses as they shouted that the troll was cheating. And they were right, Sividious knew. He'd felt the strange aura of magic as well. He could still feel it, actually, emanating from somewhere on the troll.

"What do you think it is?" Glora asked aloud, and Rommis broke off his cursing to answer.

"It's got to be a Bugwitch," he growled, "or something like it. No way a Rock Troll has those abilities or that kind of power."

"But Bugwitches are illegal," Glora complained. "Not to mention expensive. How did the Rock Troll get one?"

Rommis glanced pointedly at the tower of box seats rising beyond the darkened obstacles. "How do you think?" he muttered. "The Kaladan."

The bark-faced creatures sitting in front of Sividious and Jackie turned around to glare at the young man. "Dangerous words," one of them snarled. "Perhaps I should report your blasphemy to an Agent."

Rommis exchanged looks with Glora, then made a small gesture with his hand. Sividious felt a tremor of magic, and the two bark-faced creatures slammed together. The crack of their heads colliding echoed down the row of spectators, but no one seemed to pay it any mind. The bark-faced creatures slumped together and lay still, and Rommis returned to his conversation as if nothing had happened.

"I'm telling you," the young man insisted, "the Kaladan or their bloody, stinking Agents gave Lazacor a Bugwitch. It's the only explanation for what he is able to do." He made an angry fist. "I can feel its power even now, searching for Aya, readying another strike."

Sividious could feel it too. He could feel it as distinctly as he'd felt the young man's use of magic on the bark creatures. He could feel it as surely as he'd felt Aya's use of magic during her battle with the Dragon Centipede. And he thought he knew why. What Glora said next deepened his suspicion.

"Every creature with Shael'hala abilities can feel it as well. How do the Kaladan think they can get away with such blatant cheating?"

Rommis frowned. "They cheat all the time. Why would today be any different?"

"Well, for starters, there are many Shael'hala here today," Glora said, her eyes scanning the darkened obstacles for some sign of Aya. "And the majority of them are rooting for the Kelsprite. They won't take kindly to her being defeated in a rigged match."

"No they won't," Rommis agreed as he watched for Aya to reappear. "But by the time the Shael'hala are able to do anything about it, the match will be over. If Aya loses, the Rock Troll will be exposed as a cheater and punished. You know bloody well the Kaladan won't stand up for him. They'll let him take the heat for their actions, then they will apologize for Aya's unfortunate death and move on to the next match. If Aya wins, the Shael'hala will likely let the incident slide."

When Glora and Rommis fell silent, their eyes still scanning the darkness above the playing field for some sign of Aya, Sividious pulled out the handheld and typed the words *Shale Hala* into the search program. A little message window appeared with the question, *Did you mean Shael'hala?*

He clicked yes then read the description. "Shael'hala: A sorcerer from a Type Two or Three world who possesses the ability to sense when magic is being wielded by others. Shael'hala also have the ability to sense the magic inherent in a variety of inanimate objects. *See also:* Talismans."

"That's you, isn't it?" Jackie whispered, her eyes locked on the handheld. "You're a Shael'hala sorcerer. That's why you could feel what Aya and Shoar were doing."

Sividious nodded, and the admission made it difficult for him to breathe.

Jackie put her hand on his arm. Her eyes were intense as she asked, "Does that mean you can also use magic?"

"I don't know," Sividious told her.

But he did know. He knew as surely as he knew that he lived. He could use magic. He didn't know exactly *how* to use it, or even what he would do—he just knew it would be possible if he tried. He shook the thought away. "And I don't think I want to find out."

Jackie nodded as if she thought not trying would be best, then glanced back at the handheld. "So, what's a Bugwitch?"

Sividious typed it in. "Bugwitch: A tiny, sorcerer-like insect from the world of Tromador. Bugwitches are parasitical shape-shifters that attach themselves to their hosts in order to harness and enhance both their own and their host's magical abilities. Prolonged exposure to a Bugwitch's influence often results in death to the host creature."

"Lovely," Jackie muttered, and Sividious frowned as he tucked the handheld away.

"So now what do we do?" Jackie asked.

"The only thing we can do," Sividious said. "We watch."

The crowd was growing restless as they waited for Aya to reappear, and a chorus of boos could be heard from those cheering for the Rock Troll. In response to the boos, Aya's fans began chanting her name. Within moments, the entire stadium echoed with the sound of "Aya! Aya! Aya!"

Down on the playing field, the Rock Troll howled his anger and stomped about, smashing walls and obstacles with his cudgel. Secreted somewhere on the troll's body, the Bugwitch probed the darkness overhead with its magic, searching for Aya. Sividious could feel the tendrils of magic as they snaked among the obstacles.

A heartbeat later the Bugwitch attacked, and Lazacor raised his cudgel to send a burst of fire lancing high into the darkness. It sprayed off the edges of a large diamond-shaped obstacle, filling the uppermost reaches of the darkness with a dozen streamers of deadly heat.

Aya's slender form dove for cover behind a lower obstacle, her wings pulled in tight against her body as she spiraled down and out of sight. The Bugwitch's fire pursued her but was turned aside by a thrust of shimmering magic hurled by Aya. A nearby obstacle was shattered by the collision of magic, and fragments of steel and stone rained downward, thudding into the arena floor in clouds of dust and grit.

The Bugwitch struck again, and again Aya dove for cover behind a lower obstacle, somehow managing to avoid the deadly fire as well as the blades and spikes sticking out from several nearby obstacles. Over and over this happened—the Bugwitch lashing out with its dark magic and Aya doing her best to avoid it by diving even lower.

Sividious stiffened in horror when he realized that each attack brought Aya nearer the Bugwitch and its arsenal of magic. The little Kelsprite was quickly running out of things to hide behind. One more descent and she would be below the protective cover of darkness.

Aya must have realized the danger as well, because she went on the offensive. Hurling a torrent of white-hot fire, she turned the area around Lazacor into an inferno, driving him to his knees and knocking the shield from his hand. Then, while the Bugwitch absorbed the attack with its own magic, Aya winged her way higher, angling toward a large inverted pyramid just visible against the backdrop of stars. She landed on top of the obstacle, and Sividious felt her magic cut off as she attempted to hide once more.

The Bugwitch snuffed Aya's fire with a surge of magic, and Lazacor lurched to his feet again. He bent to retrieve his shield then lumbered forward, howling his frustration and smashing walls and pillars with his cudgel.

Fueled by the Bugwitch's power, Lazacor raised his cudgel, and a burst of dark magic exploded upward. Many of the weaker obstacles shattered, deadly missiles of steel and stone that ricocheted through the darkness above in a rumbling of thunder and sparks. Some of the missiles struck the arena shield, and rings of blue energy rippled outward from the strikes. The spectators beyond flinched in surprise. Chunks of stone and steel rained onto the playing field like debris cast from the clutches of a tornado, and Lazacor threw his head back and laughed as the Bugwitch's magic shielded him from injury.

As the rain of debris subsided, a shard of metal trailing a length of blue silk appeared from the darkness. It stabbed the ground not far from the Rock Troll, and the crowd gave a collective gasp of horror when they realized the length of silk settling around the metal shard had been part of Aya's gown. It didn't take the eyes of an eagle to see that it was wet with blood.

Sividious's heart sank when he realized what it meant, and tears formed in his eyes. Next to him, Jackie was crying openly as she stared at the strip of blue silk.

All across the stadium it was the same. The crowd went still as they watched the Rock Troll move to claim the token of his victory.

* * *

Fighting the dizziness threatening to overwhelm her, Aya wiped the blood away from her face and peered over the edge of the pyramid-shaped obstacle. Her vision was blurred, and spots of light danced inside her head, but she could still see well enough to spot Lazacor standing among the rubble on the arena floor. He was howling in triumph at his perceived victory and seemed oblivious to the debris falling around him.

The thought gave her an idea, and she hurriedly removed one of the strips from her tattered dress. Working quickly, she hooked the strip of cloth on a piece of ruined metal and dropped it over the edge. It struck the ground not far from Lazacor, and the length of silk settled around the metal like a pool of her own blood. She heard the crowd go silent.

Crawling to the center of the obstacle, she searched for its control panel and was pleased to discover that one of Lazacor's missiles had partially torn it open. Being a creature of magic, she wasn't familiar with all the inner workings of technology, but she knew enough to realize that its power source wasn't all that different than some of the kinds of magic she'd faced the past several weeks. Power was power, she knew. And without it, things ceased to function.

Pulling the panel the rest of the way open, she picked up a chunk of stone and hefted it above the array of circuitry and switches. Her injured arm screamed in protest, but she knew she wouldn't have to wait long. She also knew that Lazacor would let her know when it was time to strike.

* * *

Sividious watched through tears of anger and sadness as the Rock Troll bent to retrieve the length of blue silk that had been part of Aya's dress.

Hoisting it above his head, the vile creature howled in triumph, waving the length of silk like a banner.

The crowd booed mightily then cut off in surprise as something large and black appeared out of the darkness directly above the troll. A massive, inverted pyramid plunged downward like an arrowhead, sleek and silent.

Lazacor's fans shouted a warning, but the troll was so intent on his victory that he never even looked up. The side of the massive wedge caught him across the back of the head, flinging him forward onto his face and sending his cudgel and shield flying. The walls and pillars scattered about the arena shook from the obstacle's impact. Lazacor lay as if dead.

For a moment, no one seemed sure about what had just happened. The entire stadium looked on in silence as the winner of the Jomon final lay facedown in the dirt.

And then something tiny and blue appeared out of the darkness, spiraling downward like a wounded bird. The membrane of one wing was torn nearly in two. The other was pockmarked with holes both large and small. Blood streaked the side of her face, and her right leg had a nasty gash on it. Her dress hung about her slender form in tattered strips.

But she was alive.

The crowd erupted into thunderous cheers as the little Kelsprite landed near the Rock Troll and bent to remove something from the back of its neck. It was the size of a baseball and shaped like a tick, and Sividious knew instantly that what Aya held was the Bugwitch. He didn't know if it was alive or dead, but since he didn't sense any magic emanating from it, he assumed the latter.

Aya's words confirmed it. "Not only did I defeat Lazacor the Rock Troll," she told the crowd, "but I destroyed this creature as well. I do not know what it is, but I know it enhanced Lazacor's abilities greatly. In light of the Rock Troll's cheating and the defeat of both of these creatures, I claim victory in the Jomon Worlds of Magic Tournament."

As the crowd erupted into cheers, the overhead lights clicked back on, and the floating obstacles began retreating back into the stadium. A blue platform tracked by a dozen spotlights floated in from a side passage and moved toward Aya. It stopped in front of her, and she stepped up onto it then braced herself as it lifted her high into the air.

The stadium's video screens flared to life with live images of Aya, and grand music filled the air as the floating platform moved about the stadium so the spectators could admire their champion.

Down on the field, Lazacor was helped to his feet by a dozen Agents and escorted away. Sividious didn't want to know what the Kaladan had in store for the poor creature, but he decided death in the arena would have been merciful. No sooner had the Agents and the troll exited the field than the entire arena floor began to sink deeper into the stadium. It lowered a good thirty feet before splitting in two down the middle and retracting into the stadium's sublevels. Almost immediately two halves of a new playing field emerged from a different sublevel, merged into one, then rose to form a new arena surface. Free of everything but a carpet of short green grass, the new arena looked like a football field without the yard lines.

There was an audible boom as the new playing field locked in place, and Aya's platform landed in the center of it.

"Citizens of the universe," the now familiar voice of the stadium announcer said grandly, "I give you Aya the Kelsprite, winner of the Jomon Worlds of Magic Tournament."

The crowd went wild with cheering, and the announcer was forced to wait patiently until it subsided.

"And so," the announcer continued once it was quiet enough to do so, "it is with great pleasure that I bestow upon Aya the Kelsprite all the rights and privileges associated with Free Agent status and invite her to return to the upcoming Tournament of Champions."

"Like that will ever happen," Sividious mumbled then watched as Aya limped toward the exit amid the deafening cheers of her adoring fans. When he was certain which tunnel she was going to take, he nudged Jackie.

"Come on," he said. "Let's go make sure the Kaladan give her what she has earned."

30
TOURNAMENT OF CHAMPIONS

SIVIDIOUS AND JACKIE HAD JUST reached the concourse exit when a burst of trumpet music filled the stadium. Long, loud, and triumphant sounding, it was followed by the voice of the purple-faced announcer welcoming everyone to the Tournament of Champions. The crowd cheered wildly. Sividious and Jackie turned to stare at one another in disbelief.

"They wouldn't dare," Jackie said, but she could tell by the frown on Sividious's face that he wasn't so sure. She followed his gaze up to the video screens and found the female announcer smiling over the crowd.

"As you know, the Tournament of Champions is open to all those who have earned Free Agent status by winning a lesser tournament. Additionally, it is open to any individual wishing to pit their skills against our proven champions. This is intended to be a nonlethal match, but serious injury or death can result from participation. The fatality rate of the last Tournament of Champions was 22 percent. Therefore, all civilian participants must sign a waiver releasing the stadium of liability."

When the announcer paused to let the crowd consider her words, Jackie took Sividious by the arm. "Is this for real?"

"Afraid so."

She tightened her grip on his arm. "Why would anyone voluntarily compete?"

"Remember the Intergalactic Immunity status I told you about?" he asked. "This is how you get it."

"The prize for victory," the announcer continued, confirming Sividious's words, "is Intergalactic Immunity and all the rights and privileges associated with it. The price of failure is forfeiture of Free Agent status and loss of Free Agent rights and privileges."

"And that's assuming you aren't killed," Sividious muttered darkly. He glanced at Jackie. "This place is really messed up. The sooner we get out of here the better."

"Competitors may compete individually," the announcer continued, "or may form teams of five or fewer. If a team wins the tournament, Intergalactic Immunity will be awarded to the player with the most points."

"Points?" Jackie scoffed. "How do you score points?"

"Probably by killing someone," Sividious grumbled. "Come on, let's go find Aya."

"I don't think that will be necessary," Jackie said, pointing to the playing field.

Sividious followed her gaze to where Aya was limping back into view. Behind her, just visible in the shadows of the tunnel, stood three Agents of the Kaladan.

"What in the—something's not right, Siv! Are they forcing her?" Jackie asked, her voice heavy with despair.

Sividious nodded. "Something's definitely not right. Aya's too injured to compete and she knows it. She would have told the Agents to shove—"

"We have our first competitor," the announcer said. "Let us welcome Aya the Kelsprite, champion of the Jomon Worlds of Magic Tournament."

The crowd cheered, but it sounded different than before, nervous and uncertain.

"Our next competitor," the announcer said, talking over the cheers, "is Rogashar the Shulmite, champion of the Euripid Technology Tournament."

Wrapped in body armor that shimmered and faded as if wrapped in the heat waves of a desert mirage, Rogashar made his way toward the center of the field. The visor of his helmet was down, hiding his eyes, but when he glanced toward Aya, his malevolent smile was visible. He had a large chain gun mounted on a pivot attached to one hip. An array of pistols and grenades in various holsters graced the other. To Jackie, he looked like a Halo warrior on steroids.

"How is that guy supposed to be part of a nonlethal match?" she wondered aloud, but Sividious shook his head.

"I don't know, but I'll bet he isn't the worst of those the Kaladan invited to eliminate Aya."

He was right. The competitors kept coming, some magical, some technological, and each one more terrifying than the last.

Jackie watched ten or twelve more appear, then she and Sividious started for the tunnel where Aya had entered the field. Something had forced her to enter the tournament, and they needed to find out what it was.

As they made their way through the stadium—dodging other patrons, weaving their way down a private stairwell, and then sprinting down the emptiness of a high security hallway—they listened to the enthusiasm in the announcer's voice as she introduced each new contestant. Jackie lost count after thirty.

They were nearing the entrance to Aya's tunnel when an Agent stepped from a side passage to confront them. "What are you doing down here?" he hissed. "Those wishing to enter the tournament must—"

He was cut off as Jackie shot him in the chest with her zobo stick, knocking him backward into the wall with a sickening thud. He crumpled into a heap and lay still.

Sividious scowled at her. "You shot him too soon," he grumbled. "I wanted to hear what he was going to say."

"Sorry," she said, not the least bit apologetic. "But I'd rather not take any chances with these scumbags." She tucked the zobo stick back inside her tunic then stepped forward and nudged the Agent with her toe. "Look on the bright side," she added. "I didn't kill him."

Sividious withheld comment. Instead, he motioned toward the tunnel. "I'll go in first and distract the Agents," he said. "This one thought I wanted to compete; maybe the others will think so too."

Jackie shook her head. "We go in together. They won't be expecting to be attacked, so we should be able to walk right up to them. And two weapons at close range are much better than me trying to shoot them from a distance."

Sividious nodded. "Together, then," he said, and they rounded the corner into the tunnel.

At the far end stood four Agents. Three of them were looking out into the arena. The fourth sat on a crate, holding the arm of a tiny Kelsprite. A miniature version of Aya, the little Kelsprite was obviously a child. He was also the spitting image of Aya.

So that's how they forced her into the tournament, Jackie thought, her anger flashing into rage unlike any she'd ever felt. She glanced quickly at Sividious to find him looking equally angry.

"You take the one watching the child," he whispered. "I'll get the other three."

Jackie nodded, and they continued forward, walking right up to the Agents before any of them realized they were there.

"Excuse me," Sividious said. "I have come to enter the tournament."

The Agents turned to stare at him in disbelief. "That isn't allowed here," one of the Agents said then stiffened in surprise as Sividious raised his laser gun.

"Are you sure?" he asked, firing several rapid bursts that sent the three fish-faced creatures toppling to the floor.

Jackie shot the fourth Agent in the head then quickly took the frightened Kelsprite child in her arms and hugged him tightly.

"It's okay," she soothed. "We are here to help you."

"Aya," the child said, pointing out into the arena. "Help Aya."

"You got it, little one," Sividious said, turning toward the arena.

"Wait a minute!" Jackie hollered. "Where do you think you are going?"

Sividious took a quick breath. "Like I told the Agents," he said, forcing his voice to remain calm, "I'm entering the tournament." He tossed her the handheld. "But in case things go badly, use this to get yourself and the kid home. I've left instructions on the menu page."

Panic took Jackie by the throat, squeezing so hard she felt as if she couldn't breathe. "Sividious, don't you do this!" she screamed, but it was too late. He'd already stepped out into the arena.

* * *

The Tournament of Champions was already underway when Sividious exited the tunnel, and the clash of technology and magic was unlike anything he had witnessed in the stadium so far.

Plasma bolts from Rogashar's chain gun ricocheted in all directions, deadly spears of white-hot energy that tore holes in anything not shielded by magic or technology. Streamers of fire and stabs of bluish lightning arced every which way as various magic-wielders went on the attack. Bubbles of shimmering fire marked the places where other combatants were taking shelter. One such bubble of protective magic was the target of Rogashar's fierce attack. And there, crouched beneath it, her small frame trembling from the effort, was Aya.

Sividious pulled out his zobo stick and activated the weapon's energy shield feature. It wrapped around him in a glowing sphere that dampened the noise of battle and gave everything around him a silvery appearance.

Strong enough to repel even Rogashar's chain gun, it allowed freedom of movement but wouldn't allow him to attack unless he lowered the shield. And with death dancing all around him, he had no intention of lowering the shield.

He narrowed his eyes determinedly. If he was going to save Aya, he would have to do it with something other than the weapons he'd stolen from the Kaladan. And that meant he would have to use his magic.

Magic.

The very thought made him want to laugh hysterically.

A stream of laser fire hammered into his shield, and Sividious came back to himself in a rush. Turning toward the fire, he found an armored Halo wannabe gunning for him from atop a floating obstacle.

The man continued to fire for a moment longer then ignited his jet pack and moved to find another target when he saw that his weapon had little effect on Sividious's shield. He vanished in a swirl of greenish fire that sent several nearby combatants scurrying for cover.

Sividious turned his attention back to Aya and found her still crouched beneath her shield of magic. Rogashar was still blasting away at it with his chain gun, and now he'd been joined by two others. One, a four-armed, pig-faced creature with scaly armor, was shooting Aya's shield with four laser pistols, one in each hand. The other, a tiny reptilian creature wrapped in a shroud of darkness, was hammering Aya's shield with fists of dark magic.

Sividious closed his eyes and reached inside of himself for the magic he knew was there. Exerting all the powers of logic he possessed, he called to it with his mind, trying to reason it into existence.

No response.

He tried again, reaching for it so desperately with his mind that he thought his brain would explode.

Still no response.

He was about to try again but stopped when a sudden thought washed through him: Magic didn't come from the mind—it came from the heart! He'd been trying to understand the power of magic the same way he would attempt to understand physics or mathematics. But magic wasn't a science that could be addressed with reason and logic—it was emotional. It had to be felt!

And he could feel it, he realized. He could feel it coursing through him like his own lifeblood. It was part of him and always had been. All he needed to do was accept it.

Reaching inside once more, Sividious opened his heart to the fire burning deep inside him. He welcomed it the way he would welcome a hug from a loved one or a kiss from Jackie. He felt it the way he would feel the pain of a funeral or the death of a loved one. He felt it the way he would feel joy or fear or any of a hundred other emotions. The point was he *felt* it.

And with that final realization about the nature of magic, Sividious launched his attack, knocking the chain gun from Rogashar's grasp with a thrust of swirling, blue-white fire. Rogashar's weapon and pivot arm tore free from the techno-warrior's armor, and he went sprawling. He scrambled to his feet to retaliate but vanished beneath a barrage of laser fire before he could draw another weapon.

Turning his focus from Rogashar, Sividious reached deeper into his emotions and conjured up an invisible fist of magic energy. With a sharp jab, he punched the four-armed pig creature so hard he dented its armor and sent it hurtling halfway across the arena.

Such power, he thought then flinched as something dark struck the zobo stick's protective shield. Turning, he found that the little reptile had broken off its attack on Aya and was launching a torrent of dark magic at him instead.

Angry, Sividious readied a retaliatory strike, but the little reptile exploded into a thousand fiery bits before he could launch it. Sividious wasn't at all surprised to learn the strike had come from Aya. He found her waving to him from beneath her shield, motioning for him to join her.

When he reached her, a quick glance around the arena showed that the contest was nearing its end. Most of the combatants were either incapacitated or dead. There was still enough commotion, however, that he and Aya should be able to make a break for it.

"Come on," he said, deactivating the zobo stick's shield and weaving one out of magic instead. He had felt how it was done when he neared Aya's shield, and though his was by no means as fancy as hers, it was strong. He stretched it around her so she could let her shield drop. "We're getting out of here."

"Now?" she asked, her voice tired.

"Now," he said then scooped her up in his arms and started for the tunnel. Laser bolts and strikes of magic struck the shield as he ran, but he didn't stop. His heart was so full of emotion right now he doubted a blast from the Death Star could make it through his shield.

"But the Agents—" she said, and Sividious cut her off.

"Out of commission," he told her. "And the little Kelsprite they were holding is with Jackie."

"He's my baby brother," Aya said. "The Agents threatened to kill him if I didn't participate in the tournament."

"I figured as much," Sividious said then added, "I don't know how you managed to so thoroughly tick these people off, but they are really ticked off."

"I think they'll be much more angry at *you* now," she warned. "I hope you realize that."

"I'll worry about that after we get out of here," he said.

He raced into the tunnel to find Jackie and Aya's little brother watching from the shadows. Jackie held the zobo stick in one hand and the laser gun in the other. Three more Agents lay sprawled on the floor, and Sividious could tell by the smoking holes in their chests that Jackie hadn't used stun.

She noticed Sividious's stare and scowled at him. "Stun stinks when they're shooting to kill," she told him. "I had to defend myself."

"I didn't say anything," he said then nodded to the dead Agents. "Hand me one of their AAPs. We'll need it for Aya once we leave the stadium."

He started down the hallway, still carrying Aya. "Bring the little one," he said. "We don't have much time before this place goes nuts."

Jackie snorted. "How much more nuts could it get?"

31
A TOKEN OF FRIENDSHIP

THE MAIN CORRIDOR OFF THE arena tunnels was surprisingly quiet, but Sividious and Jackie ran as if they were being pursued by Agents. Which was pretty close to the truth, he decided, even if the Agents weren't aware of the escape yet. It would only take one to sound the alarm and the place would be swarming with the fish-faced creatures.

He glanced beside him to where Jackie carried Aya's baby brother in one arm and had her laser gun leveled before her with the other. Her face was set, but there was fear in her eyes as she nervously scanned the way ahead.

"We're almost there," he told Jackie. "We take the next passage on the left. Up the stairs and we'll exit Portal C2."

"C2?" Aya said. "What world is that?"

"Palinor," he answered as the security shield on the stairwell deactivated at his approach. He started up the stairs. "It's a Type Two world, but it is more heavily weighted toward magic than technology." He smiled down at her. "You have a lot of fans there. I sat next to some of them during your match with the Rock Troll. They felt the presence of the Bugwitch that was helping the troll cheat."

"So that's what it was," she said then shook her head. "I was very lucky to have survived. Bugwitches are formidable creatures."

Sividious grinned at her. "So are Kelsprites."

She touched his cheek affectionately. "But not so formidable that they don't need rescuing," she told him. "I owe you and Jackie my life."

"Not yet, you don't," he countered. "You can thank us *after* we get you back to your world."

They reached the landing on Level 2, and Jackie peered around the corner into the main corridor. "There's a pretty big crowd out there," she whispered over her shoulder. "But I don't see any Agents or robot police. I don't think the Kaladan have sounded the alarm that Aya is missing."

"They will," Sividious assured her. "But they'll be looking for her in the lower levels. Let's go before they run a trace on which AAPs have been used to open secured passages."

"They can do that?" Aya asked, her eyes wide.

Sividious nodded. "That's how they tracked you to my world," he told her. "But don't worry. They might be able to track us to Palinor, but they will lose the trail there."

"How can you be so sure?"

He smiled at her. "Because I'm even better with technology than I am with magic." He motioned for Jackie to proceed, and together they moved out into the main corridor.

They'd only gone a few steps before the nearest beings in the crowd stopped to stare at them in wonder. Aya brought a finger to her lips to tell them to be quiet, and most of the beings blinked in surprise when they realized what was happening. There were several, however, who shouted for someone to find an Agent.

Jackie put the nearest one down with a stun blast from her laser pistol—the others were silenced by Aya's adoring fans. "Go," some of them urged. "We'll cover for you."

Aya waved her thanks to them as Sividious turned into the passage of Portal C2 and hightailed it for the shimmering surface of the wormhole. She clung tightly about his neck as he ran. They plunged through in a flash of white and found themselves among the roots of the giant trees. Jackie and Aya's brother flashed into existence a heartbeat later.

"Can you walk?" Sividious asked.

Aya nodded. "Yes, as long as it isn't far."

"It's not," Sividious said, pulling out the handheld and powering it on. A map of that part of Palinor appeared on the screen, and he held it up as if he were using a compass. "This way," he said and started down a path between two towering roots. After a few twists and turns, he stopped at the base of a tree.

"Right here," he said then pushed the button that would activate the hyperlink. The blue scanner-like bars of light moved up the tree trunk, and a moment later the hyperlink flared to life. Aya stared at the swirl of white light in awe.

"I've connected this hyperlink to one just outside your father's castle," he told her, handing her a map he had drawn of the castle and its surroundings. "It's right here," he said, pointing to the red *X* marking one of the buildings. "The handheld described it as a basement cellar."

"It's a wine cellar," she told him. "I know the place well. It is connected to the castle by a series of underground passages."

"I know," Sividious told her. "I read about it on the handheld. It's my guess that the Kaladan have been using it to infiltrate your father's castle in order to kidnap members of your family."

"We'll put a stop to it now," she vowed. "The next Agent who comes through the link will find a nasty surprise waiting for him."

"I thought you might say that," Sividious said with a smile. "It's the reason I made you this." He handed her a stack of folded papers. "They're maps showing where each of the hyperlinks is located on your world. There are fifty of them all together."

Aya's eyes filled with tears as she took the stack of papers. "Thank you," she said. "The world of Fallisor owes you a great debt." Throwing her arms around him, she hugged him tightly.

He hugged her back as tears formed in his eyes. This was it, he realized. This was good-bye. Forever.

"I won't forget you," she whispered.

"Nor I you," he said in return. He glanced over at Jackie and found her face streaked with tears. Aya's little brother wore a somber expression as well, as if he understood the permanence of this good-bye.

Aya stepped back and looked Sividious in the eyes then took her baby brother from Jackie and removed the slender necklace he was wearing. A chain of braided gold, it bore a single polished blue stone roughly the size of a quail egg.

"This is a meyl stone," she told Sividious, holding it up for him to see. "It is the jewel worn by the kings and queens of Fallisor as a symbol of their power and authority. It is very rare and very special. I want you to have it as a remembrance of me and of our friendship."

"It's magic, isn't it?" Sividious said as Aya placed it in his hand. "I can feel it."

"It is the magic of Fallisor," she said. "A deep and powerful magic that will be with you even after you return to your own world. When you feel the magic, think of me."

"I will," Sividious told her then hugged her and her brother one last time.

Aya touched his cheek affectionately, hugged Jackie, then moved to stand in front of the hyperlink. Smiling over her shoulder at them, she tightened her hold around her little brother, stepped into the light, and disappeared.

Sividious stood silently for a moment then shook himself free of his sadness and pulled out the handheld. After programming in the new coordinates, he pointed the handheld at the shimmering surface of the hyperlink, took Jackie by the hand, and stepped into the light.

32
FINDING BALANCE

"OUR WORLD SEEMS SO DULL after all of that, doesn't it?" Jackie said as she and Sividious made their way down the game trail toward the wilderness park. They'd changed back into their regular clothes and had their disguises, the stolen weapons, and the AAPs stashed in their backpacks.

Sividious adjusted his backpack and looked around. The late afternoon sun was shining, birds were singing, and the sounds of children playing in the park below echoed up through the oak brush. To him, the world had never seemed more beautiful.

"Not really," he told her. "I kind of like it when creatures aren't trying to blast me into tiny pieces."

Jackie smacked him in the arm. "You know what I mean," she said. "Our world has inferior technology, little magic, and no awesome creatures like Aya and her brother. It really is kind of boring."

"It has you," Sividious said. "I'd say that makes our world pretty cool."

Jackie stared at him. "If you're being sarcastic," she warned, "I'll punch you in the face."

He stopped and took her by the hand. "I'm being serious," he told her then reached up and ran a finger down her cheek. "Who needs all that fancy technology and mind-blowing magic when I have you."

Jackie arched an eyebrow at him. "Uh, you didn't injure your head during the tournament did you?"

"No," he answered. "But I did learn something about following my heart." With that, he pulled her into a hug and smiled when she hugged him back.

"I love you, Jackie Molenshire," he told her as he stepped back to look her in the eyes.

"I love you too, Sividious Stark," she replied. "But don't let it go to your head."

"Oh, I won't," he told her. "My head is reserved for science. Love, like magic, has no place there."

She furrowed her brow at him. "You have that look like you know something I don't," she warned. "You want to explain before I punch you?"

"I'll explain while we walk," he said, and they started down the path once more.

"Magic is pure, raw, emotional power," he said. "It cannot be wielded with reason or logic. After all, its very existence is illogical in the first place, right? It has to be *felt* to be used. It has to be experienced." He shook his head. "Does that make sense?"

"Sort of," she told him. "At least as much sense as the laws of physics or mathematics or that theory of relativity stuff you're always talking about."

He let out a long sigh. "I suppose what it really comes down to," he said, "is that some things are understood with the mind, while others are understood with the heart."

"It's good to have both," she said. "Logic and emotion balance one another nicely." She grinned at him. "Especially when you're trying to decide whether you should punch your best friend for nearly getting you killed or if you should hug him for taking you on the adventure of a lifetime."

"I'd err on the side of emotion for that one," Sividious told her, and Jackie laughed.

"Maybe later," she said. "Too much affection all at once might ruin that scientific brain of yours."

Sividious chuckled, and they fell silent until they reached the chainlink fence separating the wilderness park from the mountain slope.

"Are you going to miss it?" Jackie asked as she jumped down to the other side. "The magic, I mean?"

"I don't know," Sividious said, staring at her through the fence. "It's hard to miss something I don't totally understand." He joined her on the other side, and they started walking again. "I can still feel it, you know. It's weak here in our world, but it is present. If I tried hard enough, I might be able to do something with it."

"You should practice on Kael," Jackie said with a laugh.

"I've already thought about it," Sividious told her with a grin. "But I don't think I will. Thrashing him with science has become a tradition."

A group of children playing hide-and-seek ran by, and Jackie watched them with a smile. "Aya's little brother was cute, wasn't he?" she said.

"Yes, he was," Sividious answered. "I can't believe Agents threatened to kill him in order to make Aya enter the tournament."

"I can," Jackie said. "They tried to kill me while I was protecting him."

"Do you feel bad about killing those three?" he asked.

Jackie shrugged. "About as bad as I'd feel about killing a coyote trying to get at my lambs," she answered. "Those jerks deserved what they got."

"I think so too," he told her then shook his head. "It's probably a good thing we're never going back. I imagine our faces will be on the Kaladan's most-wanted list for quite some time to come."

"Fugitives from justice," Jackie said coyly. "How romantic."

"Yeah, well, things didn't work out so well for Bonnie and Clyde," he told her.

"I was thinking more along the lines of Robin Hood and Maid Marian," Jackie said with a smile. "You know, with an and-they-lived-happily-ever-after ending."

"Sounds good to me," Sividious told her.

"Oh, who I am I fooling?" she grumbled. "Now that I know all those other worlds exist, I want to see them. I want to experience the wonders they have to hold. I want to go back to Pali-whatever-it-was-called and climb those giant trees."

"Who said you can't?" Sividious asked.

"But you said we're never going back—"

"To the stadium," he said, cutting her off. "I never said anything about visiting some of the other worlds through the hyperlinks." He patted the handheld tucked in his pocket. "Untraceable, remember?"

Jackie grinned at him. "And they did indeed live happily ever after," she said.

"Yes, they did," Sividious agreed. "But in the meantime, they need to finish their science projects, study for their math tests, and get their chores done so their parents don't ground them."

"Boring!" Jackie muttered.

"Balance," Sividious countered. "We can't totally ignore our lives here on Earth. This is our home, after all. Our place of logic and reason and nonweirdness. It will keep us normal."

Jackie laughed. "We're anything but normal."

"Just the same," Sividious said. "We probably ought to wait awhile before we go back to Palinor, or anywhere else for that matter. We need to give things a chance to quiet down. I don't imagine the Kaladan will forget about what happened."

"How long do we have to wait?" she asked, unable or unwilling to hide her disappointment.

"A couple months," he said. "That's half a year inside the stadium. Decades on some of the other worlds."

"A couple of months it is," she grumbled.

He put his arm around her and gave her a squeeze. "However," he said. "I understand you are doing a presentation on Japan in your social studies class. I suppose we could pay a visit to a historical site or two."

"Really?"

"Sure. What are you doing tomorrow?"

"Going to Japan with my best friend," she answered.

They walked in silence for a moment, then Jackie said. "You don't think we got the world of Palinor in trouble with the Kaladan do you? I mean, we really made it look like they were the ones who rescued Aya."

The question made Sividious miss a step. "I hadn't thought about it like that," he admitted. "I hope we didn't get them in trouble."

"What's the worst the Kaladan could do?" Jackie asked. "Lock down Palinor's access to the stadium? I'd call that a blessing, not a punishment."

"I guess we'll find out in a couple of months," Sividious told her. "There's not much we can do about it right now anyway."

"Do you think Aya will be all right?"

Sividious nodded. "I think she'll be just fine."

* * *

Later that night, Sividious pulled a large storage trunk from the back of his closet and undid the brass fasteners. Mostly full, the trunk contained everything from vacation souvenirs to old science projects to boxes of minerals and rocks. He knew it would be the perfect place to stash the items he and Jackie had brought with them from the stadium.

He wrapped the zobo sticks, the laser guns, the Agent sunglasses, and the Access Passes in a souvenir sweatshirt from Yellowstone and laid them in the bottom of the trunk next to the binder holding his *Star Wars* trading cards. He slipped the handheld inside a leather wallet and stuck it in a box with an old Nintendo DS and a Game Boy he had partially dismantled as an experiment. He didn't want it falling into the wrong hands.

That left only the meyl stone Aya had given him.

He held it up by the chain and gazed at the smooth blue stone. Its magic had weakened since coming into this world, but it was still there, a soft, ambient whisper that spoke directly to his heart and made him feel like he was something more than just an ordinary boy from Earth. Even more importantly, it reminded him of Aya.

He closed the trunk and shoved it back into the closet, then he stood and looked around the room for a place to put the meyl stone. He wanted it where he could see it but knew it needed to be inconspicuous enough not to draw Simone's attention. The little busybody would steal it.

His eyes fell on the map of the universe poster his dad had purchased for him at the Clark Planetarium in Salt Lake City last year, and he smiled. What would his dad think of his and Jackie's adventures, he wondered? Would he be proud of them for freeing Aya? Would he be upset with them for putting themselves in danger? The answer to both questions, he decided, would be yes.

He studied the poster a moment longer, and his smile deepened. Moving to his desk, he dug through a jar of junk until he found a thumbtack then stepped near the poster and pinned the necklace so the stone was centered on the map.

"I've been there," he whispered quietly, a rush of excitement washing through him, "to the stadium between worlds."

ABOUT THE AUTHOR

GREG PARK WAS BORN IN 1967 in Provo, Utah, and spent much of his youth fishing the Provo River and camping and hunting in the Wasatch Mountains with his father and brothers. In 1986, he served a two-year mission in Osaka, Japan, then attended Brigham Young University, where he received a bachelor of arts in English and a master of arts in theater and media arts.

A high school English teacher for many years, Greg is the author of The Earthsoul Prophecies fantasy adventure series. His novel *Veil of Darkness* received the USA Book News Best Book Award for fantasy in 2007. Still an avid outdoorsman, he enjoys fishing, hunting, and camping with his wife and children in Utah's backcountry.